LEGENDS

ANTHONY IZZO

CHAPTER
ONE

IT WAS time for Keppler to cut the woman's clothes off. She was in his cellar, decomposing. This was the worst part of the process. The stink would be awful. He sat at the kitchen table in the farmhouse, drinking black coffee. He was halfway through his second cup and considered getting a third.

You're putting things off.

He finished the coffee and set the cup in the sink. Then he squirted some dish soap in it and washed it. Once it was clean, he dried it with a plaid-patterned dishrag and set the cup on the drainboard.

You're stalling.

After drying his hands, Keppler proceeded to the cellar, where he flipped a switch. The cellar was underneath the entire 3,500 square foot home. His father had built a maze of hallways and rooms down here when Keppler was ten. He'd been required to help. If he didn't bring his father a tool fast enough or cut a board wrong, he got cuffed in the head. A few times, he had to duck a hammer flung at him in anger.

His father had had a short fuse. Melvin Keppler had been smart enough to lay the real beatings on body parts Keppler's teachers wouldn't see. His arms had been forever bruised. As a kid, he'd always worn long sleeves. That sucked during the summers.

His father had done the same to Keppler's mother. She would get into a bottle of cheap whiskey, belching booze fumes. His father would get angry and punch her arms and legs as she slumped in the corner of the kitchen, the whole time calling him names.

You're a worthless cocksucker. Lazy, limp-dicked weakling. You're no man. Go ahead and kill me if you think you can.

The blows would rain down on his mother. Keppler would shut his bedroom door. He was eleven-years-old at the time. It sounded like someone pounding a side of beef. The screaming and swearing devolved into soft whimpers. Keppler had no love for either of his parents, but he'd dreamed of jamming a screwdriver through his father's eye socket and watching him twitch as if shocked.

One night in his twelfth year, Keppler's father had broken his mother's nose. It was two days before Christmas. The cops came and hauled his father to jail. He saw his father only two more times after that, both during prison visits. Years later, another inmate bashed his father's skull in with a wooden table leg. Keppler felt nothing for his father's loss. He would've danced on the man's grave if given the chance.

After his father's death, his mother lived in a whiskey bottle. Keppler found her dead on the bathroom floor a few weeks after he turned twenty-two. He'd come home after working a shift as a machinist to find her blue-faced and stinking up the bathroom. She'd passed out and choked on her own vomit.

The house was his after that. To his surprise, his parents had a will, and he inherited everything, including the 400 acres they owned.

The extra land had come in handy with his pursuits.

He navigated the basement, ending up in a room that functioned as a storm cellar. Normally, he kept it padlocked from the outside. Because his quarry had expired two days ago, he'd unlocked it. No chance of escape with the woman dead. In the storm cellar, he had four, fifty-gallon drums lined up. Using a hand-truck, he wheeled it through the cellar to his special room.

He took keys from his pocket and unlocked the padlock, which secured a thick chain to the door. Inside, he flipped on the lights. The woman, whose name was Jill Cordova, according to her ID, lay on a sturdy table he'd built. He'd built it years ago.

He unfastened the woman from the table. After taking a knife from a nearby table, he cut off her clothes. She stared up at him. He'd cut a smile in her throat. Looked like hungry mouth to him. After removing her clothes, he picked her up and stuffed her in the barrel. Some things snapped inside her. No matter. She easily fit in the barrel. One reason he liked petite women.

The rest of her clothes were in a backpack upstairs. He'd grabbed her at a rest stop. He'd gathered she'd been hitchhiking. A dangerous proposition with people like Keppler around.

He threw the clothes inside the barrel. It was important that he sent them to the grave naked. Leaving as they'd come into the world.

He put the lid on the drum and wheeled it to the storm cellar. Keppler had installed a small ramp leading to the outer doors. He pushed them open and muscled the barrel up the ramp. His size was an advantage when moving barrels and bodies.

People had always stared at him. Six-foot-nine and three hundred pounds, he knew he was a freak. His mother, in one of her drunken binges, had told him as much.

You nearly tore my insides out, Richard, ripped me wide open when you were born.

As if she'd had to push out a six-foot-nine baby.

Outside the storm cellar, he muscled the drum into the bed of his pick-up. Then he hopped in the cab. A rutted road led through the woods behind his property. No one came up here, which was good for him.

He drove for a bit before reaching the grave he'd dug. Still had a shovel standing up in the dirt. He parked and hoisted the barrel from the bed. Then he shoved it into the grave he'd dug. Sweat trickled down his back as he filled in the hole. It was mid-October and cool. The damned sweat made him feel as if he'd run a mile.

Once the grave was filled in, he headed back to the house. In an upstairs bedroom, he removed the woman's spare clothes from her pack. He was careful to empty out pockets and check tags for no signs of identification. Satisfied the clothes looked generic enough, he headed to the cellar and threw them in the washer.

While the clothes washed, he would take a shower and get the stink of death off himself.

The woman's clothes had finished washing. He smelled fresh, like Irish Spring soap. Keppler had another cup of coffee. Also made himself an omelet and some sausages. After plating his breakfast, he headed down and put the clothes in the dryer.

Upstairs, he devoured the food and washed his plates. There would be no dirty dishes in this house. When he was a kid, crusty dishes had been piled in the sink. Mice had skittered along the floors, leaving droppings. Roaches climbed over the dirty dishes. Once he'd inherited the house, dishes gone done right away.

When he took possession of the house, he'd hired a cleaning woman to scour the place. She'd filled dozens of trash bags and spent hours cleaning up mouse droppings and dead roaches. His parents never threw out papers. Piles of envelopes, letters, and old receipts littered the house. Those went in a shredder. Once the house had been cleaned, he'd hired an exterminator.

A clean home also didn't arouse suspicion. Had someone viewed dishes piled in the sink and trash strewn everywhere, that would've stood out. *Ever been up to the Keppler place? It's a goddamned mess. You should see it.*

Once the dishes were washed, he grabbed the dried laundry and stuffed it in a garbage bag. He headed out to his truck and drove into town, pulling into the First Christian Church. The church's lawn was getting shaggy, and leaves had blown into the front gardens. He'd have to stop by and take care of that. He couldn't slack on his duties as church caretaker.

Next to the church was a one-story brick building that functioned as a donation center. He parked in front of the building and grabbed the trash bag filled with clothes. Inside, he spotted Mary Esteban, who ran the donation center. She was sorting through some canned goods.

"Mary," Keppler said, nodding.

"What brings you in, Richard?"

"Have some old clothes for donation."

"Wonderful. Set them over there, please," Mary said, pointing to a pile of filled trash bags. They never questioned him when he brought clothes in. He was just a good churchgoing citizen doing his part to help the disadvantaged. People could be so fucking stupid sometimes.

Keppler set the bag in the pile.

"Richard, could you do a favor for me?" Mary said.

"I can."

"There's a light bulb out in the storage room. Mind changing it?"

He did, but he didn't complain. "I'll take care of it."

He went to the storage room and grabbed a light bulb from the shelf. Didn't need a ladder. He reached up and unscrewed the dead bulb. Then he placed the new one. He didn't give two shits for the church or anyone here. He needed money. Also needed people to see him as a solid citizen.

Gacy had his clown gig. Just a friendly clown entertaining the community. The Bike Path Rapist who'd terrorized the Buffalo area had coached little league. Bundy presented himself as an average guy in need of help when he approached victims. The mild-mannered church caretaker was Keppler's thing.

The light bulb changed, he threw the old one in a trash can near the storage room. On his way out, he nodded to Mary, who was busy sorting clothes. She waved and told him to have a good day.

CHAPTER
TWO

SULLY HAD ALREADY TAKEN off in the woods. Jeremy headed into the trees that bordered their new home. Kelly was unpacking a carload and the movers were due to show up within the hour. As soon as they'd let the black lab out of the car, Sully had spotted a deer and chased after it.

He didn't know what Sully would do if he could even catch a deer. Probably lick its face and make it a friend for life. Jeremy set off down a rutted path in the woods. He could hear Sully barking in the distance.

Jeremy went a few hundred yards. He spotted Sully up ahead, and beyond the dog, a barbed wire fence strung between wooden posts. The dog had the good sense not to try and squeeze through the barbed wire. He saw no sign of the deer.

He caught up to Sully and took hold of his collar. "Was it worth it, you goof?"

The dog barked, as if to say, of course it was, you silly bastard. Jeremy spotted a large house with a wraparound porch a few hundred yards away. Gray with black shutters. A pick-up truck was parked in the long driveway.

The neighbor. He'd have to introduce himself at some point. He wanted to be friendly, but not too friendly. Maybe shoot the shit about sports or the weather. Borrow a tool now and then. He didn't want to be hanging around with the guy next door on a regular basis. Good fences made for good neighbors.

A side screen door opened and a giant of a man stepped on the porch. The guy was pro-wrestler big. He regarded Jeremy from the porch. Stood there with a mug in hand. The mug looked like a child's toy tea cup in the man's paw.

Jeremy waved. The man didn't return the wave. Just stood there, expressionless. Sully barked again. The man sipped from his cup. He waved again, thinking the guy might not have noticed the first time.

Again, the big man didn't return the wave. Maybe they wouldn't be so friendly with the neighbor. "Looks like he wants to be left alone, huh?"

Sully wagged his tail. Jeremy let go of the collar. "Trusting you, okay? No more bolting after woodland creatures."

Together, they started down the path. Jeremy glanced at the farmhouse. The man stood on the porch like some sort of monolith. He felt a little unnerved by the guy's actions. Or lack of actions. Sully hadn't barked at the guy. Maybe that meant he was okay. The dog was a good judge of people. They'd once had a plumber come to the old house to fix a leak in the basement. Sully had snarled at the guy and wouldn't stop barking.

Although Jeremy had apologized for Sully's behavior, the dog had been on to something. A week later, he and Kelly saw the plumber on the news. The cops had picked him up for burglary. Seems he was returning to customer's homes with his buddies and breaking in. They'd found boosted stereos, televisions, and jewelry in his plumbing van.

Back at the house, Kelly was lugging a box up the stairs. She spotted Jeremy and said, "Found our escapee?"

"Yeah, he stopped at the neighbor's barbed wire fence."

"Did you see the neighbor?"

"Yeah. Guy was a bit odd. Waved to him and he just stood on his porch like a monument."

"Weird," Kelly said. "Grab a box. Movers will be here soon."

Sully followed him to the SUV. Kelly had left the hatch open, and the entire back was filled with boxes. Jeremy grabbed a box marked BOOKS and hauled it into the house.

They'd purchased it at auction. It had good bones. Between an inheritance they'd gotten from Kelly's parents and savings, they'd been able to renovate it. The hardwoods shined. The smell of fresh paint lingered.

He'd picked out a room that would serve as his writing study. Kelly took a spare bedroom as her office. There was also a small apartment over the garage. They hadn't decided what to do with that yet.

Jeremy had broken through with his self-published books. He'd written a fantasy series, a military sci-fi series, and a bunch of books with a Jack Reacher-like character named Harlan Stone. Those had sold incredibly well. One of the big four publishers had gotten wind of its success and offered him a contract.

He'd politely turned it down, figuring he could make more money in the long term on his own. Plus, he'd be hanging on to his copyright. If he happened to die before Kelly, he'd already set up a literary estate so she would benefit from the books after he was dust.

He looked forward to them being home together. Her position as an IT manager allowed her to work remotely.

Over the next half-an-hour, they got the SUV unpacked. The movers arrived in the meantime and began hauling in furniture. Sully followed them around. The movers didn't seem to mind; Sully would probably hop in the truck and go for a ride. Sometimes he was a little too easygoing.

After a few hours, the movers had everything inside. Jeremy paid the bill and tipped them, and they chugged away in their truck. It was getting toward late afternoon. The shadows grew long.

"What do you say to ordering take out?" Kelly said.

"I won't argue."

"There was a little sandwich shop in town that advertised takeout. Saw it on the way through."

"Sounds good."

They locked up the house. On the way into town, Kelly looked up the Coyote Café on her phone. She ordered turkey panini with fries for them both. Sully rode in the back seat, curled up and dozing. If he was good, Jeremy planned on breaking off some turkey to give the dog. That would get a dirty look from Kelly. A little white meat wouldn't hurt him.

Kelly pulled up to the curb at the Coyote Café. A cartoon coyote wearing a jaunty scarf decorated the window.

"Hop out and grab the food?" she said.

"I'm on it," he said, and got out. As he approached the window, he noticed a flyer in the window. It was a picture of a twenty-something woman named Jill Cordova. She'd been missing for almost two weeks. It gave a brief description of her. She was twenty-eight, five-foot-one and a hundred fifteen pounds. The picture showed the woman standing in front of a huge Ferris Wheel.

He hoped they'd find her, but usually if missing persons posters were up, it was a bad sign. Jeremy headed inside. The clerk was setting a plastic bag on a table behind the counter. She had dyed green hair with the sides shaved.

"Too bad about the girl on the poster," Jeremy said.

"Been a big story around here."

"Hope they find her."

"It doesn't look good. She made a call from the rest stop on the 90. Last time anyone heard from her. Your order?"

Jeremy gave his name. The clerk handed the bag over the counter. "She live around here?"

"Nah, wasn't from town. Passing through, I guess."

Jeremy told her to have a good night and departed the café. On his way out, he took a last look at Jill Cordova's picture. Someone was worrying about her somewhere. Parents. Maybe a partner. She looked happy in the picture. He imagined whatever had befallen her had been terrible.

In the car, Sully greeted him with a low woof.

"All set?" Kelly said.

"That woman on the flyer. Looks like she was abducted."

"Hope they find her. At least for closure."

"Guess she disappeared from the rest stop we passed on the way here."

"That's a little close for comfort," Kelly said, pulling away from the curb. Jeremy's stomach rumbled. They'd driven right through lunch in order to get to the house and start unpacking.

They drove through the business district in town, eventually hitting the main road. Their house was around ten miles out of Harlow. They passed a blue sign with gold lettering that proclaimed: *Thanks for Visiting Harlow!*

As they pulled up the driveway, he saw their giant of a neighbor standing near the front steps. He watched their SUV roll up the driveway.

"That him?" Kelly said.

"That would be our neighbor."

"Maybe he's friendly, after all," Kelly said. Damn he's huge."

"Told you," Jeremy said. "Think he moonlights for the WWE."

They got out of the car. Jeremy opened the rear passenger door and Sully hopped out. Sully barked at the neighbor, inching forward, then backing up, as if not sure about the guy.

"Richard Keppler. Pleased to meet you both."

That was a far cry from the guy who didn't wave back. Maybe he hadn't seen Jeremy waving earlier. Keppler was dressed in jeans, a dark blue work shirt, and black work boots. His hair was on the long side and greasy. Jeremy put him between forty and fifty years old.

"I waved before. Wasn't sure you saw me."

"I saw you."

Jeremy and Kelly introduced themselves.

"Got yourself Coyote Café. I like their food."

"It looked good," Kelly said.

"So how long have you lived here?" Jeremy said.

"All my life. Forty-nine years. Got four-hundred acres. Almost to the county line."

"That's impressive," Kelly said.

"It's just land. You're renovating the place. Finished the floors, did you?"

How did he know that? "How'd you guess?"

"Saw the contractor's van in the driveway."

"If you need anything, stop by. I'm sure we'll be seeing you around," Jeremy said.

Jeremy hoped that would end the conversation. Keppler seemed to be meandering. He wanted to get inside and eat dinner.

"You will."

Keppler lumbered back to his truck. The engine kicked to life and Keppler pulled away. Jeremy felt an overwhelming sense of relief when he was gone. He couldn't say exactly why.

"Is it me or was he a little creepy?" Kelly said.

"It wasn't you. Relieved he's gone."

"Let's go eat. Hopefully he'll keep to himself."

"Didn't like how he was just waiting here for us," Jeremy said.

"Yeah, me neither. Maybe he's just awkward."

Jeremy shrugged. They headed inside, Sully darting ahead. He roamed around, sniffing everything. Then he gave an enthusiastic bark. The dog ran upstairs and continued barking.

"What's gotten into him?" Kelly asked.

"Sully, come!" Jeremy said.

The dog thumped around upstairs. "I'll go have a look," Jeremy said.

Jeremy headed upstairs. There were four bedrooms up there. Right now they were filled with cardboard boxes. He found

Sully in the master bedroom, where their four-poster bed had been set up. He was sniffing around the bed.

"What's up with you? C'mon," Jeremy said, patting his leg and heading for the door. Sully followed him downstairs.

In the kitchen, Kelly was unpacking the sandwiches on the island.

"What was his deal?" Kelly said.

"Doing a lot of sniffing. I found him in our bedroom."

"Maybe he smells the movers. Dig in. I slaved over this dinner," she said.

CHAPTER
THREE

THAT HAD BEEN CLOSE. The new neighbors had returned just as Keppler had left their house. His lock pick set had gained him easy access to their home. Most locks were easy to defeat, as he'd found. Some morons didn't even lock their doors. That was just asking for someone like him to come calling.

He'd taken his boots off to avoid leaving prints. Most of their things were in boxes. He considered taking a souvenir, maybe a pair of Kelly's panties. It might have been obvious had he rummaged through a box, though. Would've been easier to take them from a drawer. Or the hamper.

Going through the house had given him an electric thrill. Like the big dip on the first hill of a roller coaster. Going through people's things was a kick. Seeing their most private possessions when they had no idea he was snooping. The thrill had been diminished because their stuff was in boxes. Maybe he'd pay another visit once they were unpacked.

He parked the truck and headed into the house. Decided to learn more about his new neighbors. Inside, he sat down in the front room where he kept his laptop. He hadn't learned their last names, but he was able to look up the real estate transaction on the home at 2118 Southhampton Road. Kelly and Jeremy

Trank had purchased the home for one-hundred-ninety-six grand.

Good. Had their last name. He typed Kelly's name into Google. She had a LinkedIn profile. Director of IT at a big manufacturing company. A few social media profiles. Nothing earth shattering. Next, he typed in Jeremy's name. After scrolling down, he found an intriguing article.

His neighbor was a writer. There was an interview where Jeremy talked about his success in self-publishing. He'd authored twenty-two books. In the interview, he talked about making enough money to leave his day job and write full time.

Someone who could tell a story. *His* story. Keppler realized he couldn't do this forever. There were over twenty bodies buried out on the back 40, as his father used to call it. The humble groundskeeper routine couldn't hold up forever. And he wasn't going to prison. He'd get life, and then some.

A writer could make him a legend. Write a book about his exploits. Of course, Jeremy would need an incentive to write a book about Keppler. He could make that happen. Despite his shitty upbringing, Keppler knew he was bound for something great. His name would live forever. He'd just known that, even as a kid.

They would talk about him like the other legends. Gein. Albert Fish. The Zodiac.

A wave of excitement passed over him. Almost as good as when he brought someone down to the cellar. He had planning to do. Watch their patterns. Observe. Then wait for the perfect time to take them. He couldn't bring them here. That was far too close.

His Uncle Ray had a hunting camp where he spent most of his time. The old, drunk bastard was divorced from his Aunt Sue. He could get Ray out of the way, then use his camp. It was way out where God lost his shoes. No one would disturb Keppler.

Perfect.

. . .

This was fucking perfect. Hannah watched the asshole at the bar slip a powder into the woman's drink. She'd been watching him all night. Loud. Moving in too close to the women at the bar. Putting a hand low on their backs and buying them drinks.

He'd been chatting with a woman in a black cocktail dress. She had a poodle perm and enough makeup on to shame a clown. While she was turned and chatting with someone else, the creep had roofied her drink.

Time for Hannah to get moving. She got up from her table. Strutted across the bar. She got some looks from men. Tonight she had on a skintight, short dress. Royal blue. Normally, black was her color, but she looked damned good in this outfit. Tattoos on full display. Hair cut short. Showing some leg.

Usually the guys that approached her were average bros. Guys wearing too much cologne and cheap khakis. She wasn't interested in them. Guys like the jackass at the bar were her targets.

She sidled up to the guy. He was big. Over six feet and loaded with gym muscles. Had his sleeves rolled up and wore a nice watch. He had his back to Hannah. She touched his forearm and he turned around.

"I love that watch."

"I like your tats," he said.

"Thanks, you got any?"

"No, but I've been thinking about it."

Bullshit you have. "You should totally do it. They'd look good on you."

"Buy me a drink?"

The woman with the poodle perm took notice of Hannah and shot her a filthy look. Hannah leaned across the bar, making sure to spill the woman's drink, and said, "You're out of your league, honey. And clean that clown paint off your face."

The glass rolled and shattered behind the bar. The barmaid,

clad in a tight, black t-shirt advertising the bar – Johnny G's - grabbed a whisk broom and dustpan. The remains of the drink spread across the bar. The poodle woman grabbed some napkins and blotted up the booze.

"Fucking bitch," she said.

"Get gone," Hannah said.

"Yeah, why don't you?" the guy said.

The woman stormed off in a huff. Hannah felt like a shit for being mean to her, but the woman didn't realize how close she'd come to being a victim.

"What's your name?" Hannah asked.

"Brock."

Of course it is.

"What are you drinking?"

"Just an iced tea."

"That's no fun," he said.

"I know how to have fun."

"I'll bet," he said, giving her the up and down, gaze lingering on her cleavage.

Hannah scanned the bar. The woman with the excess makeup was nowhere to be found. Good. If she'd had a moment, she would've told the woman to watch her fucking drink. But the lady was out of danger. At least from the danger Brock the schmuck posed.

Old Brock was giving off booze fumes. His eyes were glassy. He ordered himself a straight vodka with lime. Hannah took the iced tea as soon as the bartender set it down. She held the drink close to her chest. They stood at the bar, face-to-face.

She learned he was a financial planner. He bragged to her about his clients, vodka fumes in her face while he talked. Brock Cappe worked with three of the biggest injury attorneys in the state. He had clients who worked for the Bills and Sabres.

Hannah didn't give a shit. She wanted to move things along. "I have a room close by. Want to get out of here?"

"You a hooker?"

"Just a girl that wants to have fun."

"Guess this is my lucky night."

He settled the tab and they left the bar.

"I'll drive. You look like you've had a little too much fun to drive."

"Okay," he said, staggering a bit.

They headed to Hannah's beat-up little Honda. Brock got in the passenger's seat. They ended up at a little motel off the interstate. The clerk had taken cash. It was getting hard to find places like that. Even harder not to leave an electronic trail. The clerk hadn't asked questions. Didn't even ask for a name.

She supposed it didn't matter. Her time was going to grow short, and she had work to do. She parked in the space near her room door, number one hundred seven. They got out. She entered first. The room had the smell of old socks. Water stains marked the ceiling.

"Why don't you sit on the bed?" Hannah said. "I'll get ready in the bathroom."

"Can't wait," he said, already fumbling with his belt. His crotch bulged. He lay back on the bed, stripping off his pants. Jesus, this guy was eager.

She ducked into the bathroom, taking her purse with her. In the bathroom, she stripped down to her black bra and panties. From her purse, she took a slim dagger. She left the bathroom, the dagger held behind her back.

Brock was down to his boxers. Hard and ready to go. Too bad for him.

"What do you got there?"

"A special toy."

"Nice. I didn't even have to work for this."

Hannah would have to work quickly. He was big and strong. If she let him get the upper hand, she'd be in trouble. She scooted on the bed, straddling his chest. Hannah was careful to keep the knife behind her back.

He groped her breasts. Squeezed hard. She tried not to wince.

Son of a bitch was used to taking what he wanted and being rough. "Ready for the special toy?"

He grinned. "Bring it on."

She reached behind and jammed the stiletto into his crotch. Judging from his scream, she probably hit a testicle. Before he could make more noise or buck her off him, she slapped a hand over his mouth. Then she plunged the dagger into his throat. She kept her hand plastered over his mouth.

His eyes bulged. Brock thrashed. She squeezed her thighs, holding tight. After a few moments, his eyes rolled and he stopped fighting. She kept the stiletto in his throat for a few moments, just in case he wasn't quite dead.

Brock didn't move. Wouldn't be slipping any more women date rape drugs. Satisfied he was dead, she slipped off the bed. Blood bloomed on his underwear. It made a little pool on the sheets. She pulled the knife from his throat with a wet *THWOCK*. It had left a neat little hole just below his Adam's apple.

She had blood smeared on her hand. She looked down at herself. No blood on her skin or underwear. This was the biggest risk she'd taken so far, having used a motel.

There'd been two other creeps she'd taken care of. One deep inside a state park. She'd responded to a Craigslist Ad looking to meet a woman with tattoos and a "goth aesthetic." The ad vaguely talked about fulfilling a lifetime dream. She'd met the creep, who'd told her his name was Dylan.

Dylan had a cabin rented for the weekend. Told Hannah straight out he wanted to tie a woman up and do as he pleased. Was she into that? She'd nodded enthusiastically. *You can do whatever you want. I had a good feeling about your ad.*

She'd seen his skin flush a little. Eyes dilated. Men were so goddamned easy. Before they started the festivities, she asked him to take a walk. Hannah had stabbed him three times in the gut. Once in the side of the neck. Never saw it coming. She'd pushed his body into a ravine, where Dylan ended up among the leaves.

The other guy she'd stabbed while parked in an abandoned lot in downtown Buffalo. He'd propositioned her in a bar for a blow job, thinking she was a prostitute. It was going to catch up to her soon. The killings hadn't been connected. Yet.

The hotel clerk could be problematic. He'd seen her. Even though she'd paid in cash and not given her name, he could make an ID. She had to get gone and far away from here.

In the bathroom, she washed her hands, careful to rinse the blood down the drain. She rinsed blood off the knife, and it sluiced down the drain. The knife went back in the bag. She got dressed, throwing on jeans and a flannel. Stuffed the tiny dress in the bag.

Hannah wasn't about to stay here with the now-deceased Brock. Getting the fuck out of here.

She shut the lights off. Left the room key on the table. As she headed out the door, she hung the DO NOT DISTURB tag on the door.

After throwing the bag on the passenger seat, she hopped in her crappy Honda and pulled away from the motel.

CHAPTER
FOUR

THE BANE OF HER EXISTENCE – the lump – had been found during a routine self-exam. It wasn't huge, but it was there. Hannah had made an appointment to see her primary physician. Robson Industries, where she worked in customer service, had decent health insurance. Her deductible wasn't likely to put her in the poorhouse, and most things were covered.

Still, she'd gone through the exam with a mild sense of worry while the doc poked at her. He was an elderly guy on the cusp of retirement, but he listened to her. Didn't dismiss Hannah's concerns like a lot of male doctors would have. Plus, he usually errored on the side of caution.

"Definitely something there, but probably not a concern. Likely a fibroadenoma, which are benign. I'm giving you a script for a mammogram to be on the safe side."

A week later, she had the mammogram. The news wasn't good. It was an aggressive form of cancer. Both her primary and the oncologist had given her details, a slew of info about gene types and risk factors. All she knew was she had to go through rounds of chemo and radiation. She got through that. Puked her way through chemo. Eventually wound up with a double mastectomy and reconstruction. From the ages of twenty-five to twenty-seven, she spent most of her days at Roswell Park.

A week after her twenty-seventh birthday, she rang the bell on the ward, signaling her treatment was over. She was cancer-free. The docs were optimistic. Scans and bloodwork kept coming back clear.

Until earlier this year when she'd started having abdominal pain. The cancer had come roaring back. *Ain't that a bitch?* The rotten bastard had gotten to her liver. She sat stunned as the oncologist, a kindly woman named Dr. Chen, explained that she had six months to a year left.

It was then she'd decided to right wrongs. The first guy had been an accident, of sorts. He'd pulled her into an alley while she was walking back to her car. Had been out for dinner by herself. Wanted time to chew over what the doctor had told her.

The chicken had been bland and tasteless. The glass of wine set a fire in her belly. The chocolate cake she had for dessert was sickly-sweet.

She'd been distracted and yanked into the alley. She'd struggled. Kicked the guy in the nuts. Jabbed him in the eye. It was ugly. She'd gotten hold of a brick and slammed it into his skull. Something had cracked when she hit him. He'd flopped on the concrete, and Hannah had run.

Back at her apartment, she broke into sobs. She started shaking, and it scared her when the shaking wouldn't stop. After a while, she calmed down. Debated on calling the police, but how many times had she called them when she was with Derek and they'd done nothing? And her own father. The reeking Gin breath. Groping at her with callused hands.

No, the police weren't her friends. She'd have to be careful. A part of her got a little thrill when that brick connected with the creep's head. She was ashamed of that, but the fucker had it coming. He certainly hadn't dragged her in the alley with the intention of asking for a dance.

There were creeps like him everywhere. Like her father. Like

Derek. Victimizing women. And she'd decided to become an avenging angel while she could. Before the cancer began to eat her up.

There'd be no more treatment. She'd already decided that. Had enough puking from the chemo. Constipation from the painkillers. The indignity of losing her hair – although she liked rocking the buzzed look now. It was kind of badass.

She was an only child. Dad was dead – thank Christ. Her mother had left while the bastard was still alive. Last she knew, Mom was working at a John Deere factory and shacking up with a stock car driver.

Hannah had few affairs to finish up before the cancer got worse.

And taking a few would-be rapists with her wouldn't upset anyone. At least not family members. She had none around to be ashamed of her anymore. The seed had been planted years ago. She knew she had the potential for violence. Had her father to thank for that. And the other shithead men in her life.

It started with her father when she hit puberty. A slap on the rear-end when she walked past. A pinch. A lingering gaze. She wound up spending hours in her room. Kept a chair jammed under the knob because the lock was busted. That was until he threatened to whip her with an electrical cord if she didn't remove the chair.

Lots of things were busted in their shitty apartment. Mold crept in the shower. Outlets didn't work. Her father was always going to get around to calling the landlord, but never did.

Her dad worked as a forklift operator. Mom in an industrial laundry that provided uniforms and tablecloths for their customers. Her father would hit bars on the way home, smelling of stale beer and Old Grandad by the time he got home. Mom would cook a Stoufer's entrée or something else frozen and retreat to her bedroom for the night.

That left her alone with her father most of the time.

C'mere Hannah. What, you don't kiss your dad anymore? Sit on my lap. You're getting a rump on you. Would you look at that?

Then the nighttime visits started. At first it was sitting on her bed after she'd been asleep and drunkenly rambling. His body odor and gin fumes filled the room. She would close her eyes and wish for him to go away.

The rambling monologues consisted of how he got screwed in life and could've been plant manager. The drunken nonsense then turned into him stroking her leg. It progressed to him squeezing her ass one night.

She'd kicked him, fighting back, and he'd backhanded her, splitting her lip. He'd kept her home from school for a week while the lip healed, bullshitting the school and saying she had the flu.

She started getting in trouble soon after. Shoplifting makeup. Throwing rocks at passing cars. Got in three fights at school, one where she busted a girl's nose for calling her father an alkie. The alkie part was true, and she had no love for her father, but the girl pissed her off. Anger was her constant companion. Later in life, she would attribute her hair trigger temper to her home situation.

As a teen, she'd just wanted to smash things without thought.

She supposed a therapist would have a field day unpacking her issues.

Things had changed for her a week before Thanksgiving her freshmen year of high school. She'd had enough of her father's shit.

He'd come home particularly wasted on a Thursday night. He'd won on a scratch off ticket and blew it at the bar. At first, he'd passed out on the couch after dinner. Hannah was relieved. Maybe he'd leave her alone, but maybe he wouldn't.

Either way, she was going to be prepared. After dinner, she'd swiped a paring knife from the drawer and slipped it under her pillow. He came stumbling in her room just after eleven p.m. She slid her hand under the pillow. He sat on the bed.

"I won five hundred bucks. Did you know that?"

I don't give a fuck. Leave me alone.

He placed a hand on her ankle. She gripped the knife. His hand went higher. She whipped the knife out and slashed him across the cheek. He leapt off the bed holding his face. Blood splashed on her Metallica poster. She bolted from the room. Ran from the house in her PJs to Mrs. Kowalski's house, where her elderly neighbor let her in and called the cops.

Instead of her father being removed from the home, it was Hannah that got sent to juvie. After that, she ended up back home. She was nineteen. Mom was long gone. Her father got himself thrown in prison after he drove drunk and slammed into an off-duty State Trooper. The guy had a wife and four kids. It didn't take long to convict him.

She hoped that the other inmates asked him how he got his facial scar. A guy who tried to molest his daughter wasn't going to be popular in prison.

She hadn't spoken to him in years. Once in a while she got a letter apologizing and asking her to put money in his prison commissary. Hannah ripped the letters up each time. Damn if that didn't feel good.

After she'd put some distance between herself and Brock's rotting corpse, she pulled over at a rest stop. She was near a town called Harlow. Hannah was careful to park under one of the sodium vapor lights in the lot.

The knife she left on her lap. Just in case. Locked the car doors.

She leaned against the headrest, closed her eyes, and dozed off.

KEPPLER GOT restless around eleven p.m. and decided to take a ride. The rest stop where he'd taken the woman wouldn't be busy. But the cops might be watching. A lot of fools got caught returning to the scene of the crime.

He decided to cruise around town. Maybe stop and pick up a frozen pizza at the Gas n' Go. He headed out to his truck. It had a cap over the bed. That had allowed him to stash victims unseen. He'd hosed and scrubbed it after kidnapping his last victim. Hoped he'd eliminated any trace of her.

Keppler pulled into the Gas n' Go's lot. They were open until midnight. Outside the store stood four sets of gas pumps, each covered by a canopy. He headed inside. The clerk was rearranging meat snacks in front of the counter. Squatting down. A fair amount of her ass crack showed her jeans riding low.

Keppler headed for the freezer cases at the rear of the store. He liked the Red Baron Supreme. Could down two of them if he'd wanted. Instead, he opted for one pizza. From the beverage cooler, he grabbed a two-liter Pepsi.

The clerk was now behind the counter. He eyed her as he headed up front. She was a cute brunette with a Mandala pattern tattoo poking out from under her sleeve. Petite. She'd be an easy one to handle.

This wasn't a good time or place. He'd surely been on the store's security cameras. It was bright here, and even though it was late, another customer could enter the store.

He set the pizza and Pepsi on the counter.

"Not quite a midnight snack, huh?" she said. Her nametag read Katie.

"Always had a big appetite."

"Same. I could go for tacos right now."

"I hate Mexican."

"How can anyone hate Mexican?"

"Never cared for it. I'll take pizza."

"I respect a good frozen pizza. Still not tacos."

Katie rang up the pizza and pop. She placed them in a plastic bag and gave him the total. He paid with cash and she gave back his change. She seemed friendly enough. Keppler considered himself good at camouflage. It was too bad. She would be a good candidate for the basement.

He'd keep her in mind as a potential target.

Her nap over, Hannah drove to a Gas N' Go in a town called Harlow. Her stomach rumbled. A quick snack would do her good. From her spot in the lot, she saw a guy who was defensive tackle big standing at the counter. He was chatting with the clerk.

She headed inside. The guy was even bigger up close, well over six-foot-five. He glanced at Hannah as she passed by. Got a bad vibe from him right away.

From one of the aisles, she grabbed a bag of chips and a meat stick. At the cooler, she got a bottled iced tea. She felt the guy looking at her. Did she look guilty? She had a bad moment when she thought maybe she missed washing off some of Brock's blood.

No, she'd gotten it. Had double checked before she'd left the scene.

She overheard the guy telling the clerk that he worked as a custodian at a church. Her purchases selected, Hannah got behind him in line. It appeared he'd already cashed out. A frozen pizza and two liter of pop rested in a bag on the counter.

"Maybe I'll see you again," the guy said.

"Um, sure. Can I help you?" the clerk said to Hannah, peering around the giant.

The guy turned and regarded Hannah. Got himself a good look.

"Take a picture and it'll last longer," Hannah said.

"Guess I'll be going," he said, grabbing his purchase. He lumbered out of the store.

The clerk craned her neck to peek out the window.

"Glad he's gone. Shit. He's still sitting out there."

"Was he bothering you?"

"He was friendly enough at first. Kept talking, though. I got a creepy vibe from him."

"Same," Hannah said. "You have a ride home?"

"I live alone. Just moved here," the clerk said.

Hannah couldn't leave the clerk alone. Not with that creep out there. "What time you get off?"

"I'm not into that, no offense."

"Not trying to pick you up. I'll hang around in case that creep comes back."

"I'm off at midnight. You gonna hang until then?"

"I'll be around. Just in case."

She was likely getting herself in more trouble, but she couldn't let any harm come to this woman. Avenging angel, and all. As she stood at the counter, a sharp pain lit up her side. She doubled over, holding her belly.

"You okay?"

"Yeah, I'll be fine," Hannah said, wincing. The doc said that would get worse over time. She had pain pills in her purse, but wanted to keep her focus sharp. Eventually, the pain would win and she'd become reliant on the pills. Right now, pain was on the horizon, distant. An approaching train. Eventually, she'd be in its path.

The pain diminished and she stood up.

"Hey, I'll be fine," Katie said. "You can take off."

"I'll keep an eye out."

"You're not going to do something crazy, are you?"

"We need to look out for each other is all," Hannah said.

Katie rang her purchases up. Hannah stepped into the cool night. The creep pulled out of the lot and sped away. Hopefully that would be the last of that guy coming around. She'd still keep watch and wait for the cashier to leave.

No one had looked out for Hannah. She'd make sure other women weren't left alone. In her Honda, she opened the meat stick and the drink. She bit a piece off, relishing the greasy taste.

The creepy guy was massive. You'd need a wrecking ball to take him down. Maybe she'd overreacted and he wouldn't be back to harass the cashier. She sighed and focused on enjoying her snack.

Keppler returned home and headed for the kitchen. He preheated the oven for his pizza. While he was waiting, he turned on the television. Every night, he checked for stories on the missing woman. Tonight, he tuned into the Spectrum News Channel, which ran constantly.

There was a mention of the woman. The news story showed a long shot of the rest stop. They interviewed a detective, who said they were pursuing numerous leads. A tip line had also been set up for people to leave information anonymously.

They didn't have shit on him. Wouldn't be setting up a tip line if they did. No one would suspect the mild-mannered church groundskeeper. He thought about the clerk at the Gas n'

Go. *Katie.* She'd shown interest in him. Keppler never had a girl-friend. He'd never been interested romantically in women.

He got his thrills with women other ways.

The oven beeped, now pre-heated. His thoughts turned to the new neighbors. The writer. Someone to tell Keppler's story. He'd flown under the radar for years. Why not have his name known? Not now, of course. He could have his story written and someday release it.

For now, it could be a book he could savor, look at whenever he wanted.

While the pizza cooked, he went to the bedroom and dug around the back of his closet. He reached under a pile of clothes and brought out his own book. A scrapbook that had belonged to his mother, with the word *Memories* in gold script scrawled on the front.

He sat in a recliner and opened the book. He'd collected newspaper clippings over the years. Faces of women who'd disappeared captured forever in grainy newspaper photos. There'd been candlelight vigils for them. Keppler had considered attending one, just to see the looks on people's faces, but that would've been pushing it. He flipped through the book.

He had a few locks of hair pressed under the plastic in the scrapbook. On another page, he'd placed a medallion from one of his victims that said MOM. That had been a woman named Sonny. He was careful to burn their wallets and any ID in his woodstove.

Keeping the scrapbook was risky, but it gave him an undeni-able thrill. His body of work, laid out in front of him. If it were ever found, he'd be locked away for life.

No one would ever find it. Or the book his writer neighbor was going to do for him.

The timer dinged. He placed the scrapbook on some built ins in the den. He'd put it away later.

His belly grumbled. While he ate, he'd make a plan to snatch the writer and his wife. Also had to pay his uncle a visit up at the cabin.

CHAPTER
SIX

HANNAH FINISHED HER SNACK. From inside her car, she watched Katie the clerk through the window. The woman went about sweeping the store and vacuuming the entry rug. She locked the doors and closed out her register. After a while, the lights went out and Katie stepped outside, locking the door.

She turned, aware Hannah was watching her.

Katie approached the Honda, fumbling with her keys. Hannah noticed a small canister of Mace attached to the keyring.

Fuck. She thinks I'm a threat.

Hannah hopped out of the car, putting her hands up to indicate she meant no harm. "Whoa, no need for that."

"Are you some sort of fucking stalker?"

Hannah shook her head. "I'm just looking out for you. Lots of bad guys out there."

"I don't need a babysitter. It's really creepy you hanging out in the parking lot."

She flipped the top on the Mace. Hannah didn't need a face full of pepper spray to add to her troubles. "I'll get going. Just got a creepy vibe from that guy."

"He's not here. Do I need to call the cops or are you going to leave?"

"I'm going."

That hadn't gone as expected. She got back in the car. Katie stood off to the right, the canister pointed at the car, as if to ward Hannah off. "Give it a rest honey."

Hannah pulled away, watching Katie in the rearview. When Hannah was out of the lot, the other woman retreated to her car.

She needed someplace to crash for the night. When the cancer had returned, she'd set out on the road, leaving her apartment behind. She'd told the landlord she had to go out of state for medical treatment. Had paid the rent six months in advance.

Life had turned into sleeping in cheap motels and her car. It was just a matter of what would catch up with her first: the law or the cancer. The cancer was a given, but she would elude the law for as long as she could. She didn't want to spend her remaining days rotting in a prison infirmary.

She drove through the business district in Harlow, passing an assortment of restaurants, a library, a post office, and a single-screen movie theater. Past the movie theater, something caught her eye: a used car lot. Out front sat a small RV. It looked vintage. An orange and brown stripe graced its yellowing sides.

The price was within her budget. She had some money in a savings account. Enough to purchase the vehicle. There was a Key Bank up the street. Perfect. The RV would give her a place to sleep and stay out of motels. She'd stop by and do business with them in the morning.

She turned down a side street, rolling past a park. A basketball court in the park was illuminated by sodium vapor lights. The street hit a dead end near a field. She supposed this was as good a spot as any. Parking in the business district might draw attention from a passing cop car.

Hannah parked, killed the lights, and climbed into the back seat. She hit the key fob and locked the doors. She had a pillow and blanket stashed on the floor. After setting up the pillow, she wedged herself onto the seat and put the blanket over her.

Now to try and get some sleep.

CHAPTER SEVEN

JEREMY STEPPED ONTO THE PORCH, enjoying the crisp morning air. He had a cup of dark roast in his hand. They'd set up a few folding chairs out here. He could imagine them getting a couple large rockers for the porch eventually. He and Kelly could sit out here in the late summer and watch the sun set while crickets hummed. That seemed ideal. Maybe he'd even put in a fire pit.

He took a seat in one of the folding chairs. His thoughts returned to Keppler. Why had the guy been waiting here for them? That was pretty damned odd. And was he poking around the house?

Plus, Sully had acted weird when they'd gotten inside.

Kelly stepped out on the porch, Sully following her. Jeremy dismissed his worries as paranoia. Kelly wore a University of Buffalo hoodie. Hair up in a messy bun. Sully ambled over and nudged Jeremy's hand, tail wagging.

"Good morning to you too," Jeremy said, scratching Sully behind the ears.

"Mind if I join you?"

"I reserved you a seat."

Kelly sat down. She had about an hour before she started

work. Jeremy would get to writing soon after. He'd write from around eight a.m. until noon, take lunch, and then answer any emails and take care of things like book marketing and website updates. Then it was a few more hours of writing before dinner.

"Our new neighbor is unique," Kelly said.

"Kind of. Strange he showed up here waiting."

"Got kind of a vibe from him."

"Same," Jeremy said, sipping his coffee. "Hopefully he keeps to himself."

"We can only hope."

"Think he was snooping around?"

"Could be. Sully acted funny."

Kelly said, "We locked the doors."

"True. Maybe we're being paranoid."

"Too many true crime podcasts."

He wanted this to be their little paradise. Away from the city, where they'd had an apartment. Their car windows had been smashed multiple times. Someone had jiggled the doorknob on the apartment door when Jeremy was watching television one night. He'd had the door locked. By the time the cops had shown up, the would-be intruder had fled.

There'd been gunshots a few times. Drunks yelling. The occasional junkie passing out on the sidewalk. He was glad to be out in the country, away from the chaos.

"We're probably being paranoid after living in the city," he said.

"I just hope he keeps to himself."

"We're home during the day, so the house won't be empty. Plus, we have our intrepid dog guard here."

"Sure," Kelly said. "If we need someone to snuggle an intruder to death, Sully's a good candidate."

"I saw a bakery in town. How do you feel about some pastries?"

"I could handle that."

"I'll finish my coffee and make a run."

"If they have cinnamon rolls, I wouldn't be opposed to one."

"You got it."

Hannah awoke to light filtering in the car. She sat up and massaged her neck. Sleeping in the car sucked. Her back felt like someone was wringing her muscles out. A trip to the car dealer to check on that RV was in order.

As she folded the blanket up, she got another ripping pain in her side. She closed her eyes and tried to breathe through it. The pain passed after a few moments, but damn if that didn't hurt.

It was only going to get worse. That terrified her. She wasn't necessarily afraid of death. Didn't believe in an afterlife or any type of supreme being. It was her opinion that no god would let a parent do the things her father did to her. If that god existed at all. And if he allowed it, God was a son of a bitch. She'd tell him to his face if he did exist and they met someday.

The pillow and blanket stored, she got out of the car. Stretched again, and got behind the wheel. She drove past the park, where some crows meandered on the grass, strutting and pecking. A sign of death, crows. They were carrion feeders. Would they be able to smell her impending death, the rot within her?

Jesus, you're morbid Hannah.

She cruised by the car dealership. The windows were dark. She had a few hours before they opened. Her stomach groaned. There was a restaurant called Chet's up the street. The sign out front advertised a breakfast special for $7.99. Couldn't beat that with a baseball bat.

Hannah proceeded to Chet's and pulled in the lot. While parked, she took out her phone. She searched the local news websites until she saw it: *Body Found in Motel*. They had a description of her but no name or car. Thank Christ for that.

The motel clerk had been lazy. That would buy her a little

time, but it was only a matter of time before someone identified her. The tattoos and the buzzed hair stuck out.

She couldn't buy a vehicle, after all. Or go in the diner for breakfast. Which meant she'd be living in her car for a while. A couple of construction workers in Carhartt overalls came out of the diner. They passed by the car. She felt as if they were staring, even though they'd barely glanced at her.

Harlow was twenty miles from the motel where she'd killed Brock. She should've taken him in a back alley, given him the hope of getting a blow job, then knifed him. Dammit. Too late now.

She pulled out the lot. Reminded herself to take some deep breaths. As she drove through Harlow, it felt like everyone on the sidewalk was staring. A woman with a stroller. A guy jogging in a hoodie and short athletic shorts. The Waste Management guys tossing trash into the back of their truck. All glaring at her.

Hannah focused on the road. Glanced at the speedometer. She kept it at twenty-eight. Not speeding, but not slow enough to attract attention. Another spasm ripped through her side. She fought through it, steering with one hand. The other hand was pressed against her side.

The pain faded and she passed a sign thanking people for visiting Harlow.

The town in her rearview mirror, she sped up a little. The speed limit sign ahead indicated 45 was the limit.

No speeding. Easy. Think of where to go.

Nothing came to mind. What had she gotten herself into?

Keppler rose early and headed to Chet's for breakfast. He was always an early riser and enjoyed the dark before dawn. As a kid, he'd had to pack his own lunch. Usually baloney on semi-moldy bread. He'd always broken the moldy pieces off. If he were lucky, there'd be some mushy apples in the crisper drawer.

Now, he could eat like a damned king. Hell with his parents. In the booth at Chet's he ordered a tall stack of pancakes, an omelet, and two sides of bacon. He shoveled the food in, chewing with his head down. He was aware of people casting glances at him, watching him dine with ruthless efficiency.

Between shovelfuls of food, he slurped coffee. When he was done, he belched and wiped his mouth.

The television mounted above the counter played a news story about a body found in a motel room. Twenty miles down the road at a place called the Garland Motor Lodge. What caught his attention was the description of the woman who'd rented the room.

The police were looking for a woman with close-cut hair. Heavily tattooed and about five-foot-three. That sounded an awful lot like the woman who'd been behind him in line at the Gas n' Go. Not that he was going to report her. The last thing he needed was interaction with the police.

The waitress dropped the check on his table. He left a twenty-dollar bill and headed out. As he was heading to his truck, he spotted the writer across the street. He was coming out of the bakery with a white bag in hand.

JEREMY HAD PURCHASED two cinnamon rolls, plus a few croissants for he and Kelly. He stopped to reach in his pocket for his keys. That's when he felt someone watching him. Across the street, in the diner parking lot, stood Keppler.

Dammit.

Jeremy hurried down the street, where he'd parked in front of a barber shop. From the corner of his eye, he spotted Keppler crossing the street. Coming diagonally in Jeremy's direction.

"Hey neighbor," Keppler called out.

Jeremy couldn't be a total dick and ignore him. He turned and said, "Hey Richard. Didn't see you."

"I think you did."

"Just heading back home."

"Got some baked goods I see."

"That's right."

An awkward pause. He felt like Keppler was sizing him up somehow. His breath rattled in his throat, as if he had phlegm stuck.

"Well, I should get going."

"You're a writer."

"That's right. How'd you know?"

"Word gets around."

Or did you do some digging on me?

"What kind?"

"What kind what?" Jeremy said.

"What kind of writing do you do?"

"Fiction. Little bit of everything."

"Ever do a biography?"

"Can't say that I have."

"That would make you some money, I bet," Keppler said.

"Not really my thing."

"Still. A biography of a famous person. Bet you'd make millions."

This was as bad as the time someone told him he should write his own version of *Fifty Shades of Gray* and become an instant millionaire. "Probably won't happen. I'll stick to fiction."

"What'd you get from the bakery?"

"Cinnamon rolls."

"For you and your woman?"

Your woman. That was an odd way to phrase things. In addition, Keppler didn't gesture when speaking. His hands stayed glued to his side. "For me and my *wife.*"

"You probably have a lot of writing to do."

"Yeah, pretty busy. I'm gonna head out."

"Good luck with your writing today."

Jeremy thanked him and hurried toward the car. He wasn't a fan of small talk, and making conversation with Keppler made him flat out uneasy. He got in the vehicle and set the bag on the passenger seat. As he pulled away, he looked in the rearview mirror.

Keppler was still standing there, watching him drive away.

Hannah felt some small relief as she left town. The county road was flanked by woods. She wanted to stop somewhere to get her thoughts together. Somewhere private. Up ahead, she spotted a road that wound through the trees.

She turned on the dirt road. Up ahead, she spied a cabin. There was a rusting boat trailer parked next to the structure. There was also a pair of ATVs under green tarps. She stopped the car. She'd hoped this would've been a plain old dirt road where she could collect her thoughts.

There was no car parked at the cabin, and the windows were dark. She supposed she could sit here and fake being lost if anyone came along. The RV idea had been foolish. Making a large transaction would've gotten her caught. She was just so damned tired of funky-smelling motel rooms and sleeping among fast food wrappers in her car.

At least it was quiet in the woods. She could have some peace for a few moments as she pondered her next move.

She rested her head against the steering wheel. Closed her eyes.

Something tapped on the windshield. She turned and saw the barrel of a shotgun pointing at her. A lean man with stubbly cheeks held the gun. "Step out of there."

For a moment, she pondered starting up the car and speeding away. She reconsidered. Her odds against escaping a shotgun blast were not good.

Shit.

She stepped out of the Honda. The man took a step back. He was sickly thin, his cheeks hollowed. A sour smell came off him, a combination of sweat and cheap whiskey. It was a stink she recognized all too well, having smelt it on her father for years.

Great. She'd run into a drunk with a gun.

"What you doing on my property?"

"I got tired driving so I decided to rest."

"You got tired driving this early in the morning?"

"I've been driving all night."

"This is private property."

"We've established that."

"You some sort of smart ass?" the man said.

"I'll get in my car and head out. How about lowering the gun?"

"Don't tell me my business. We're gonna walk up to my cabin and have a chat," the man said.

That shotgun barrel looked huge. He didn't have much meat on him, but he was a full head taller than her. Had veiny, strong-looking hands. Deceptively strong. Plus, she'd have to get past the gun. She could make her move at some point. Just not now.

He waved the shotgun, indicating she should head for the cabin. Reluctantly, she went, and he followed.

Her knife was in her bag. In the damned car.

Smoke rose from a stovepipe on the roof. The tang of woodsmoke filled the air.

"Go on in. The door's open. I'm about to have breakfast."

She stepped on the covered porch and opened the door. It was basically a one room structure. Kitchen on one side. A woodstove and some ratty furniture on the other. There was also a small bathroom.

On the small kitchen table rested a plate with two runny eggs and a piece of toast.

"Have a seat at the table."

"I'll stand."

"Sweetheart, you never argue with a gun."

"The name's Hannah, *Sweetheart*."

"Look, I ain't gonna hurt you. Just have a seat."

"Lower the gun first."

He seemed to ponder this for a moment. His lips moved, but no words came out. Ultimately, he lowered the shotgun. She sat at the table, across from the plate with the toast and eggs.

"If you're polite, I'll make you some food."

The eggs and toast didn't look that appetizing, but she couldn't deny the hunger pangs digging at her belly.

He leaned the shotgun in the corner behind him, where the counter met the wall.

"What's your story?" he said, snatching up a paper napkin from the table. He took a seat. Then he unfolded the napkin and tucked it into his shirt collar, creating a bib.

"I'm heading to my parents' house in Erie."

"You from around here?" he said, picking up a fork. He cut into the egg and poked a forkful. It went in his mouth. Some of the egg ran down his chin.

"Downstate."

"Hmmm."

"I told you my name, what's yours?"

"Ray."

"You live here year-round?"

"Since I lost my house, yeah. Used to keep this as a hunting and fishing camp. Sold the boat years ago."

"Just you here?"

"My wife left years ago. Got a nephew in Harlow. Don't see him often, though. You hungry?"

She was, but runny eggs and soggy toast didn't seem appetizing. "I just want to get going."

"Sit and visit. Keep an old man company."

"You always force company to stay with a twelve gauge?"

"You were trespassing," Ray said. "At least have coffee. Then you can get going."

She could probably bolt out the door before he could get the gun, but did she really want to chance it? "I could go for a cup."

Ray worked at his eggs, slurping them up. He wiped his mouth, then crumpled the napkin up and tossed it on the plate. He took it to the sink and turned on a stove burner, where a percolator sat. She'd never actually seen someone use one of those.

"Hope you like jet fuel. I drink it strong."

"Whatever."

She looked around the room and didn't spot a television. Old Ray didn't seem the type to be on a smartphone, either. If he even had one. That meant maybe he was oblivious to the fact that he was harboring a fugitive.

"Yeah, I think you should stick around," he said.

"Is this your first kidnapping?"

"You can leave eventually."

Ray had his back to her. This could be her chance. She leapt out of the chair. He began to turn. She kicked him behind the right knee. His leg buckled. Hannah jammed her fingers into his eyes and he howled. That brought him to his knees. She smashed his head against the edge of the counter. He grunted and crumpled to the floor.

She kicked him in the face until something cracked. Blood flecked the kitchen floor. She stepped back, breathless. Ray's eye was swollen shut. Nose was a mashed mess. He was still breathing. Jesus, maybe she'd gone overboard. But the fucker had kidnapped her at gunpoint.

She had to get out of here.

Hannah went to the door. That's when she heard a vehicle approaching. Someone coming up the driveway. They'd see her car.

A pickup truck came into view. No way she could run out the door without being seen.

She looked around the cabin. The only place to hide was the bathroom. It was the john or nothing. Hannah entered the bathroom. There was a shower stall obscured by a curtain with sailboats on it.

Hannah whipped the curtain aside and stepped into the stall. She closed the curtain, aware that this might be the shortest game of hide-and-seek in history.

She stood in the darkness and waited.

Keppler had been able to maneuver his truck around the Honda parked in Uncle Ray's driveway. Strange that someone had parked there. Ray wasn't fond of visitors. He parked the truck near his uncle's rusting boat trailer. The place looked like a goddamned junkyard. If the old bastard died, Keppler didn't want the responsibility of cleaning up the property.

Keppler would bet those ATVs didn't run. Ray had sold his boat years ago. He mostly came up here to get hammered. Even Keppler's meth head aunt didn't want Ray anymore. She'd left him years ago.

Keppler got out of the truck. Woodsmoke rose from the pipe. Ray was here. He'd be easy to handle drunk. He could stash the body out back somewhere. It would suit what he needed while he used the cabin.

He stepped on the porch. Stood at the front door, where he knocked. "Uncle Ray?"

Keppler put a hand on the knife he had in a sheath on his belt. His untucked shirt concealed the blade. No one answered, so Keppler opened the door. When he stepped inside, he saw Ray lying on the floor. Someone had smashed his face. One eye had swelled shut.

Blood had pooled on the floor, and was that a tooth in the puddle? His breathing was ragged, but he was alive. Keppler knelt near the old drunk. Uncle Ray opened his good eye.

"Who did this?" Keppler said, taking note of the shotgun leaning against the wall.

Ray muttered something. Blood bubbled from his swollen lips. "Are they still here?"

Ray mumbled again. He wasn't making sense. "I need your cabin, Ray. Need to get you out of the way."

Keppler slipped the knife from the sheath. He was doing Ray a favor. The old man's life was pathetic. He slapped his hand over Ray's mouth. Then he drew the knife across Ray's throat, sawing through the windpipe. Ray's good eye bulged. He choked and gasped, struggling against Keppler's hand.

Keppler held his head steady. Keppler pressed his knee on the old man's chest, just to make sure he didn't squirm away. Didn't need any additional mess on his hands.

When Ray was still, Keppler removed his hand and stood up.

Now to figure out who'd beaten Ray in the first place. Only one other place to hide in the cabin: the bathroom. Unless the person took off somewhere. But why would they leave the car?

Keppler approached the bathroom door, then paused. He listened for a moment. Didn't hear anything. He stepped in and flipped the light switch. Behind the shower curtain was a shape. He'd found the intruder.

CHAPTER
NINE

WHEN THE LIGHT CAME ON, Hannah knew she was cooked. She saw the man's form through the opaque curtain. She decided to go for the element of surprise. She whipped the curtain open and sprang from the shower.

When she saw him, she gasped. It was the giant from the Gas n' Go, and he had a knife that looked as big as a machete. Hannah attempted to slip past him, but he hip-checked her into the wall. Her teeth rattled. He grabbed her shirt and dragged her out of the bathroom.

She clawed his hand, but he wasn't letting go.

"Interesting finding you here."

There was the shotgun in the kitchen. It might be her only hope. She tried to pull away. He jerked her back and forth. He could fling her across the room without a problem if he wanted.

Hannah spied Ray's body. His throat was a bloody mess. He smelled worse dead than he had alive. His bowels had given way when he died. Hannah kicked the giant in the knee. It had no effect.

He tossed her to the floor. She banged her elbow, pain flaring up her arm. She was near the old, plaid couch that smelled like a dirty sock. Hannah got to her feet.

"Did you do that to Ray?"

"He's a fucking creep. He held me at gunpoint."

"Uncle Ray *was* a piece of shit."

If this guy was willing to kill his uncle, what chance did she have? "You're his nephew?"

"He was my father's brother."

"Why did you do kill him?" Hannah asked, hoping to buy time.

"I need this place."

"For what?"

"None of your business."

"You going to kill me too?"

"I can't let you leave."

So it was die trying to escape or let him do awful things to her. She was a real shit magnet when it came to men. Hannah's best bet was the shotgun; it was ten feet away. First, she'd have to get past him. "What's your name?"

"Richard."

She charged him. He raised his arm to slash, but she kicked him in the crotch. It was enough to give him pause. "Damned bitch," he said through gritted teeth.

Hannah leapt over Ray's body and grabbed the shotgun. As Richard turned, she raised the gun and fired. It bucked, jackhammering into her shoulder. The blast tore Richard's sleeve to bits. He howled in pain and dropped the knife. Blood bloomed on his sleeve.

She bolted for the door, pushed it open. Still had the shotgun. She glanced back. Behind her, Richard stomped around in the cabin. The blast had been enough to slow him, but not enough to kill.

At least she didn't have to worry about him calling the cops. She made it to the Honda. She set the shotgun in the back seat, then flung herself in behind the wheel.

Hannah started it up and peeled out, turning right on the

county road. She could add shooting someone to her list of crimes.

A one-woman crime spree.

Keppler's right arm was molten lava. He took off his shirt. His ears hummed from the shotgun blast. After taking a glance at his arm, he breathed a sigh of relief. There were two pellets lodged under his skin. Thankfully, Uncle Ray had used birdshot. Would've been worse with double aught buckshot.

He'd let a witness get away. Although if it was the woman who was wanted for the motel killing, she wouldn't be calling him in. Right now, he had to take care of his arm.

He rummaged around the cabin and found a small first aid kid. That would do. He examined the wound again, confirming two pellets had lodged under the skin. Not deep.

He went to the stove and turned on a burner. The propane flame popped on. After wiping off his knife blade with a nearby paper towel, he heated the tip of the blade. Then he went in the bathroom, using the mirror to guide him while he sliced into his arm. The flesh sizzled. He managed to dig the pellets out, and they dropped in the sink.

The son of a bitch thing bled for a bit. He reheated the knife and cauterized it the best he could, leaving his arm a burned and bloodied mess. He went back to the living room and opened the first aid kit. Squirted some antibiotic salve on it, and slapped on gauze and tape.

Now to take care of old, dead Ray.

Keppler stepped on the porch to have a look around. The cabin was well-hidden by the woods. No one would be nosing around. The danger would be someone coming up the road. He prayed for no visitors.

Satisfied that no one would see, he went back inside and stared at Ray's corpse. Ray had been a mean son-of-a bitch. His favorite term of endearment was "dickhead." Didn't matter who you were. If Ray was mildly upset, you were crowned dickhead. OR if he wanted another beer.

Quit running around like a little dickhead and get me a Pabst from the fridge, Ritchie.

He hated being called Ritchie. It was Richard. On more than one occasion, he'd had fantasies of slipping some drain cleaner in Uncle Ray's beer. Of course, he would've had to pop the tab first. *Here you go, Uncle Ray, I opened it for you. Hope your fucking throat bleeds.*

That was in the past. Now the useless old fuck was dead, and Keppler had a place to operate. He grabbed Ray's ankles and dragged him out of the cabin. Ray had a small shed out back. Keppler hoped to find a shovel in there.

He hauled Ray around back, leaving his corpse and entering the shed, where he found a rusted spade. There was also an axe, a push mower, and shelves filled with everything from wasp spray to lighter fluid.

Keppler grabbed the spade and found a flat spot in the woods free of tree roots. He dug down around three feet. Took him a bit and sweat trickled down his brow. Then he dragged Ray to his final resting place and rolled him in. Covered him up.

You're fertilizer now.

Keppler smoothed out the dirt, then piled leaves and sticks over it. Then he smoothed those out, trying to make it look natural.

No one would be up here. That was in his favor. Uncle Ray had no friends. None of the family bothered with him anymore.

Back inside, he grabbed some paper towels and found a bottle of all purpose cleaner under the kitchen sink. He did his best to wipe up the blood, then stuffed the bloody towels in the trash. He'd take care of those later. Then he shoved the trash can under the sink.

He spotted a key ring with two keys hanging on a nail. He assumed those were the cabin keys. Keppeler tried them in the front door, and they worked the deadbolt. Good.

Now to head back home, shower, and dispose of his clothes. His pants had bloodstains on the knees from scrubbing.

Things were falling into place.

Hannah found a parking spot in a mall one town over from Harlow. The Westport Galleria. Unlike a lot of malls these days, this one seemed to be thriving. She parked at the far end of the lot, away from the building. Hoped that would allow her some anonymity.

Her breathing now steady, she turned and looked in the back seat. The shotgun sat on the floor. She grabbed the blanket from the back seat and tossed it over the shotgun. She should've left it behind, but her focus had been on running to the Honda.

Richard had said he needed the cabin for something else. Killing other people up there? He was capable of murder, that was clear.

On her phone, she pulled up the web browser and put in Ray's name and the town. Raymond Keppler, sixty-eight years old. There had been a tax lien on him at one point. He owned the cabin property. Ray's name also came up on a foreclosure in Harlow.

While she was reading, a hot pain shot through her side again. She rested her head on the wheel, holding her side. They were getting worse. The pain pills were calling her name. She considered popping one and resting in the car.

No, not yet. She needed to be sharp.

Once the pain had passed, she typed in *Keppler, Richard. Harlow, New York.* She was betting on Ray and Richard sharing the same last name.

An address in Harlow came up for Richard. He also came up under a church directory. Interesting. She clicked on the website, where his picture popped up. *Richard Keppler, Custodian.* It was a headshot of Keppler. He had on a blue work shirt in the photo.

His hair was shorter, cut into a buzz. She wondered about the age of the picture.

A churchgoing killer. Unless he wasn't still there. He looked relatively the same in the picture. There was one way to find out if Keppler still worked there.

She risked a call to the church.

The phone rang three times. A woman answered, and in a cheerful voice, she said, "First Christian Church, this is Ellen."

"Hi Ellen. I spoke to your custodian about doing some repair work at my house. I've lost his number. Would you be able to give it to me?"

"Richard? Of course. One sec."

"I have his number here. Are you ready?"

She opened the notes app on her phone. "Go ahead."

Ellen gave her Richard Keppler's name and phone number.

"I really appreciate that Ellen."

"He's so helpful. Doesn't say much, but he does a ton for this church."

"That's what it's all about," Hannah said.

"I agree. Have a blessed day."

"You too," Hannah said, ending the call. Another search gave her Keppler's address. Keppler had something bad planned. It would be in her best interest to skip town, but something drew her to Keppler. Maybe she'd crossed his path for a reason.

It couldn't hurt to drive by his house. Just a quick pass and then she'd be on her way.

"HE TRACKED you down outside the store?" Kelly said.

They were seated in the breakfast nook, both with fresh cups of coffee. The cinnamon rolls rested on a plate between them. "He came from the diner parking lot."

"You don't think he followed you?"

"I think it was coincidence. Still uncomfortable."

"What did he say?"

"Asked me about the writing. Seemed interested in it."

"What specifically?"

"He wanted to know if I'd written any biographies."

"Odd question," Kelly said.

"Consider the source."

"Do you think he's dangerous?"

"Creepy, but not necessarily dangerous," Jeremy said.

"Watch yourself in town," Kelly said.

"I'm a big boy."

"Yeah, but he's bigger."

"Let's make these rolls disappear. I've got to get back to work," Jeremy said.

Sully barked at the front door, his tail wagging.

"He's gonna need to go out," Kelly said.

"I'll take Sully duty when I'm done with my roll," Jeremy said.

He hoped Keppler wasn't outside again. He'd had all the interaction he could stand for a while. Jeremy hadn't heard a truck outside. Probably just a routine bathroom trip for the mutt. Still, he'd check out the window for any sign of his odd neighbor before heading out.

Just one peek at Keppler's place.

She headed back to Harlow and followed the GPS on her phone. She'd put in Keppler's address. The houses were sparse on this road. She passed a large ranch home with horses grazing behind a split rail fence. More trees. Then she spotted the mailbox by the road. Had Keppler's last name on it.

Hannah slowed the vehicle, getting a glimpse of a crisp, white farmhouse at the end of a long driveway. The pickup truck was parked near the home. Behind the house, she spotted a barn.

She sped up, not wanting to linger.

A deer bolted in front of her. She swerved left, smacking the deer's hindquarters. A black Labrador ran into the road and she jerked the wheel hard left. The car juked onto the shoulder, and she slammed the pedal, bringing it to a halt.

She glanced at the road. The lab barked and trotted back toward a nearby driveway. A bearded man of around thirty-five appeared at the driveway's edge. "Goddammit Sully!"

He noticed Hannah's car and she saw him mouth *Oh Shit*.

He hurried to her door and knocked on the window, as if she couldn't see him standing there.

"You okay?"

Hannah nodded. She waved him away from the door so she could get out. Sully followed his owner to the car, tail wagging. She stepped out.

"He spotted a deer. From the look of your front end, you clipped it."

"It bolted right in front of me."

"Sully chased him. Shit, I feel awful about this."

"Not your fault."

Sully approached Hannah, nuzzled her hand. She scratched the top of the dog's head. She'd wanted a dog as a little girl. Hannah's father had told her she'd probably kill it somehow. Sully moved closer and nuzzled the side of her leg.

"You made a friend," the guy said. He wore a flannel shirt and jeans rolled up at the bottom with expensive-looking boots. Struck Hannah as a guy who'd be into craft beers and the Lumineers.

"What's his name?"

"Sully."

"Good boy Sully, just stop chasing those deer. I have to go."

"You're leaking fluid. Don't think you're going anywhere," he said, pointing at the car's front end. The front left had been smashed in. Steam curled from the radiator. Fluid dripped from underneath the car and pooled on the shoulder.

Fuck.

"Have Triple A?"

"Can't say I do."

"I'm new. Just moved in, but I imagine there's a garage or two in town. You want to come up to the house? My wife and I can at least offer you something to drink while you wait."

What the hell to do? If she chose to wait outside, it might seem odd. She still had the knife in the bag for protection if this guy turned out to be a creep. "Let me get my bag out of the car."

She fetched her bag. This put a crimp in her plans. She couldn't very well sleep in the car now. She'd have to call the insurance. Get a rental. Get it towed. Christ, what a pain in the ass. Maybe Mr. Beard here would give her a ride.

"I didn't catch your name," the guy said.

"Hannah. You?"

"Jeremy. Follow me."

· · ·

Jeremy's wife was a pretty brunette named Kelly. She'd put coffee on and welcomed Hannah. They both apologized again for Sully chasing the deer in front of her car. She couldn't be pissed at the dog. A dog is gonna be a dog. Intentional or not, she was screwed without a car.

They shared some amazing cinnamon rolls with her. Some of their stuff was still in cardboard boxes stacked around the house. She wondered if they'd met their neighbor yet. If they knew what he was all about.

"You from town?" Kelly asked.

"Just passing through. I grab odd jobs here and there."

She told them she'd been living out of her car. Sold her possessions after taking care of her mother for three years. The dementia had finally taken old mom. It had put such a strain on Hannah that she'd sold all her stuff and hit the road. She was amazed how easily the lies had come, and the couple had nodded and expressed sympathy.

She felt shitty for lying, but the truth was going to stay buried. And hopefully they didn't connect her to the killing at the motel.

"My grandmother has dementia. Horrible," Kelly said.

"It's been a long few years," Hannah said.

"So losing that car sucks for you," Jeremy said.

"Puts a dent in things, yeah."

She'd have to call the tow truck. No idea where she was going to stay the night. Supposed she could find a motel, but that would mean registering. She couldn't bet on another lazy clerk who would bypass her ID. "Gotta find a place to stay."

"I think there's a motel in town," Jeremy said.

"You said you do odd jobs?" Kelly said.

Where was this going? "Yeah."

"We could use a dog walker, someone to take Sully out while we're working," Kelly said.

"I don't really have a place to stay."

"There's the spot over our garage. There's a space heater and a bed."

This was soon. But she didn't have any other options. It might be okay for a bit. Stay out of sight. "I could use a place to crash. And I think Sully likes me."

"Great. It's the least we can do for your car getting wrecked."

"Wasn't your fault, really," Hannah said.

"Still. At least until your car's fixed," Kelly said.

She could always run in the middle of the night if she had to. And it would be running. Literally. "Sounds good."

"How's two hundred a week for walking the dog?"

"Sounds fair. But I'm not going to be around long."

"We'll take the help," Jeremy said.

"Looks like I'm a dog walker then."

Hannah had the car towed. Jeremy gave her a ride into town to a garage called Guy's Auto Service. She called the insurance and reported it. Sent the agent some pics of the damage. He assured her no problem. She'd have the vehicle back in a week.

That was a whole week she'd be stuck here. Right now, all the cops had was a description of her. So far, no photo of her had been circulated, and they hadn't tied the description to her name. Hopefully she could stay under Kelly and Jeremy's radar until the car was ready.

When they got back, Kelly showed her to the room above the garage. Hannah had brought her bags and managed to wrap the shotgun up in a blanket and a quilt from the trunk.

The room had a metal-frame bed, a nightstand, a desk, and a boxy television on a stand. "Bet I could watch the A-Team and the Golden Girls on that."

That drew a laugh from Kelly. "I'll bring some fresh linens. That space heater should work fine."

"I appreciate this."

"Appreciate you walking Sully."

"He seems like a good dog."

"He is. Just a little too curious for his own good."

"We'll get along fine," Hannah said. "You meet your neighbors?"

"Just the one. He's a bit odd."

Hannah feigned surprise. "Oh yeah?"

"We found him waiting around for us. And he tracked Jeremy down in town."

"Sounds like a stalker."

"I'm hoping he stays away," Kelly said. "Kind of gave me the creeps. You can use the bathroom in the house, obviously. It's off the front hallway."

Kelly left her alone in order to go get fresh linens. Hannah sat on the mattress. It was old and dusty, but there were no stains. She checked her phone, searching for news on the motel murder. The victim had been officially identified as twenty-seven-year-old Brock Talbot of Tonawanda, NY.

Police had set up a tip line for anyone who had information. Hannah played a video from Channel Two in which Brock's tearful parents asked people to come forward. Brock's mother said he was a good kid who worked hard. Funny how parents didn't know their kids. Brock the date rapist. All American shithead.

The news reporter rattled off a description of Hannah.

Hannah had kept her tattoos covered with long sleeves. The short hair matched the description, but there were tons of women with her hairstyle.

She turned the television off.

She was getting bored. Decided to head to the house and see if she could walk Sully. She knocked and Jeremy answered the door.

"Hope I didn't disturb you," she said.

"Was just between chapters."

"You're a writer?"

"Guilty as charged."

"What do you write?"

"Sci-fi, fantasy, and some thrillers."

"That's cool. Sully need walking? I'm looking for something to do."

"Sure. C'mon in."

She stepped inside. Sully came bounding out to greet her. Hannah knelt and stroked the dog's side. Her early life would've been so much better if she'd had a dog. Maybe there would've been some refuge from her parents in a pet.

Jeremy brought a harness and leash out, then got Sully rigged up for the walk. He handed Hannah the leash. He grabbed her a plastic bag for cleaning up crap, and then they were off.

She walked Sully down the driveway. The dog was polite. Excited, but he didn't tug on the leash. She turned left, away from Keppler's house. A stiff breeze blew in her face. There was a taste of winter in that breeze.

Sully stopped and sniffed. Lifted his leg and peed.

Life almost felt normal walking a dog.

CHAPTER
ELEVEN

KEPPLER BALLED up his bloody clothes and stuffed them in a trash bag. His hair was still damp from the shower. After the shower, he'd scoured the tub to eliminate any traces of blood. He'd throw the clothes in the regular trash. You could toss a body in the trash and the waste disposal company wouldn't bat an eye. They didn't pay attention, and his clothes ending up in some random landfill didn't worry Keppler.

His time at the house was coming to an end. If he was going to snatch the neighbors, he couldn't come back here. Maybe he'd take his show on the road. After his story was written, he'd use his talents elsewhere.

He had a few things to purchase. Keppler had noticed an old RV for sale at the lot. That could serve him well. He liked the idea of becoming a killer on the road, like in that old song.

Keppler headed out to the truck and drove to the Home Depot in the next town. He was a regular there, purchasing things for his job at the church. They wouldn't bat an eye. In the Depot, he purchased some duct tape, thick rope, pliers, a hammer, and a blow torch. He used the church credit card to pay for them.

When he was done at the Home Depot, he drove to the car lot

in town. The RV was still there. No surprise, as it had seen better days. He got the attention of a salesman, a tanned, blonde guy in a polo and khakis. The salesman introduced himself as Dylan.

"What can I do for you today?"

"That RV. I'd like to buy it."

"It's in great shape. Wanna have a look inside?"

"How does it run?"

"Like a champ," Dylan said.

"I don't need to see inside. Let's talk price."

"Sure. C'mon in and we can chat."

They dickered back and forth on price. Dylan went back to his manager's office a few times. Keppler got the vehicle for a thousand dollars under asking price. They took care of the paperwork. He was going to come back later with a cashier's check and pick up the vehicle.

He'd have to walk into town to pick up the RV. Couldn't very well ask the neighbors for a ride.

Keppler drove out of town, heading back home. As he was coming up the road to his house, he spotted the woman. She was walking his neighbor's dog. Had her head down talking to the mutt at her side. He knew her. That short haircut stood out. No doubt it was the woman from Ray's cabin.

He passed her. She hadn't noticed him. That was interesting. What the hell was she doing walking the neighbor's dog? Were they friends? If she'd truly killed that guy in the motel, she'd keep her mouth shut about Keppler. No way did the woman want the police coming around. He wouldn't have to worry about his neighbors finding out.

She hadn't seen him. That was the important thing.

He had to stay focused. That was never his strong suit in school. Keppler had constantly been scolded in school for staring out the window in class. For not completing in-class activities. *How do you expect to get ahead in life, Richard?* That had been the mantra of his seventh-grade teacher, Mr. Shackford. Shackford with his cigarette breath that he tried covering with wintergreen mints. He'd had fantasies of bashing in Shackford's head with a hammer.

He was going to amount to something. Once he went through with this plan, he was going to be mentioned in the same breath as Bundy and Gacy. Shit, they kept making movies and about those guys and discussing them on podcasts. Eventually, he'd send the book about his exploits to every true crime website and outlet he could find.

His notoriety would continue. Taking the show on the road. Popping up and terrorizing communities, then disappearing into the night.

First, he had to get Jeremy to write the book.

When to carry things out? Nighttime would be best. Catch the neighbors sleeping. He could slip in using the lock picks. The dog might be problematic. He'd have to work around that.

The connection with the woman from the cabin still puzzled him. He still had a throbbing arm to remind him of his encounter with her. Payback would be a bitch if he came across her again.

Hannah had made fast friends with Sully. The lab had followed her to the room above the garage. Jeremy and Kelly hadn't seemed to mind. She'd borrowed one of Jeremy's books, an action thriller called *Blood Games*. It had one of those Jack Reacher-types kicking ass and taking names. She'd plowed through it, although it wasn't typically her type of book. The guy had a real talent for telling a story.

It was after six p.m. when she put the book down. Kelly knocked on the door soon after. She brought Hannah a plate of roast beef and mashed potatoes, along with a bottled water. Hannah thanked her and asked if Sully could sleep with her tonight to keep her company. Kelly said that was fine and made a joke about Sully being a traitor.

Once her dinner was finished, she took the plate back to the house. She read for a few more hours and took Sully out to do his business. Then she decided to turn in a little after nine. The sooner she got through the week, the better. She wanted to get back on the road in a hurry.

As she lay in bed, Sully curled up on the floor, another pain hit in her side. Like someone knifing her and driving the blade up into her ribs. She closed her eyes and winced. It was longer this time. Sweat beaded on her forehead.

The pain pills were calling from her bag. Maybe she'd take one. She got out of bed and grabbed the bottle from her bag. Took a pill and hoped it would help. After she lay back down, the meds kicked in. The pain in her side dulled and she slipped into sleep.

Keppler checked the items he'd stuffed into the duffel bag. He had rope, duct tape, rags, tools, and a blowtorch. Along with those items, he had a .38 special that had belonged to his father. He never asked where dad got it, and it was far from legal. It would get the job done, though.

He'd walked into town earlier and picked up the RV. It had grimy blinds, which would help shield his activities. It ran well enough. Had fake wood paneling and a stained orange carpet inside, but it was functional.

Now, the RV waited for him in the yard. He had one more item in a bulky case: a typewriter. He also had a ream of paper. The typewriter had belonged to his mother. She'd always had illusions about writing the Great American Novel. As far as Keppler knew, she'd never gotten past scribbling an outline on a legal pad.

While he was in town, he'd also withdrawn three thousand dollars from his savings account. That would be enough to get him going on the road. Now, it was almost one in the morning. He sat in his living room staring at the clock.

It was time to go. His targets were likely asleep. He'd cruise past just to make sure lights were off.

Keppler had also packed a bag with clothes and toiletries. After shouldering both bags, he locked up the house for the last time. Hopefully he'd be long gone before anyone came snooping around the house.

Outside, he threw the gear in the RV. Hopped in and started it up.

He cruised down the road passing the house. No lights were on. He turned around down the road and circled back.

As he approached Jeremy and Kelly's driveway, he killed the lights. He parked at the end of the driveway to minimize the chances of them hearing the vehicle. He double checked his pocket and confirmed his lock pick set was in there.

The revolver was jammed in his waistband.

Keppler crossed the lawn. No sign of movement in the house. Good.

He padded up the porch stairs, eased the screen door open and took out his pick set. So far, no barking dog. If the dog started barking, he'd rush in and overwhelm them.

Once he picked the lock, Keppler eased the door open. The bedrooms were upstairs. The couple's was the first one on the left. He inferred that from the presence of the four-poster bed in the room.

Keppler started up the stairs. He entered the bedroom. Both of them lay on their sides, back-to-back. The smell of sleep breath filled the room. He'd seen no sign of the mutt, which was good for him.

He pulled the revolver and went to Jeremy's side of the bed. For a moment, he watched the man sleep. A runner of saliva leaked from Jeremy's mouth. Keppler pressed the gun hard against his temple. Jeremy opened his eyes and blinked a few times.

"Don't scream. Don't move."

"What?"

"I've got a gun to your head. Don't want to kill you, but I will if I have to."

Jeremy was still on his side. His gaze flicked upward, trying to get a look at Keppler. "I'm going to step back. Wake your wife up. If she screams, she's dead."

Keppler took a step back, pointing the revolver at Jeremy.

He rolled toward his wife and shook her shoulder. "Babe. Wake up. Babe."

She rolled over, eyes half opened. She spotted Keppler sand her mouth opened in a ring of surprise. Keppler put a finger to his lips. "Shhhh."

"What's happening?" Kelly said.

"Get up," Keppler said. "No sudden moves."

He eyed their phones, one on each nightstand flanking the bed. While keeping the gun on them, he snatched up the phones and stuck them in his pocket.

Kelly sat up and rubbed her eyes.

"You're going to get up and get dressed," Keppler said. "Make it quick. Then we're leaving."

"Where are we going?" Jeremy said.

"Clock starts now. Get some clothes on."

Keppler stepped back, keeping the gun on them. They staggered out of bed and fumbled around. Jeremy picked up some clothes off the floor. He was in boxer shorts.

He sat on the edge of the bed and got dressed. Kelly went to the closet, stripped out of her pajamas, and grabbed a sweater and some jeans. She got changed at the bedside.

"All right. Move."

He ushered them to the front door, where they put on boots. Then he marched them down the driveway, following behind with the gun.

"Get in the RV and lie on your bellies."

They reached the RV and stepped inside. Both of them flopped face down on the carpet. This was going well so far.

"Hands behind your backs, ankles crossed."

"Why are you doing this?" Jeremy asked.

"You'll see. Help me out and you'll get home alive."

Both crossed their ankles. Keppler grabbed the duct tape, binding Kelly's wrists, then Jeremy's. Then he did their ankles. For good measure, he slapped tape over their mouths.

They shouldn't give him any trouble. He'd be able to drive without worrying about being attacked from behind.

Just to be safe, he cut a piece of rope and looped it between the couple's upper arm, binding them together. He tied it tight.

"There. You've been joined. It's official."

Keppler got behind the wheel and started up the RV. He backed out of the driveway and hung a right. Now to get them to the cabin.

TWELVE

HANNAH HEARD the distant rumble of an engine. How far away was it? Sully stood at the window, barking. Her head felt fuzzy and her mouth felt like she'd chewed sand. She smacked her lips a few times and sat up.

What was the dog barking about?

Hannah went to the window to see an old RV pulling out of the driveway. Looked like it had been new when Reagan was president. It resembled the one she'd seen in the car lot in town.

"That's fucking weird."

The RV sped away. Its lights were off.

She supposed it could've been turning around in the driveway, but that didn't jibe. Something felt off.

"Stay here, boy. I'll be back."

Hannah headed outside, rounding the house to see the front door wide open. Two huge, muddy footprints were left on the steps. As she approached the porch, she spotted more prints leading up to the door.

"Shit," she muttered.

She ran back to the apartment and grabbed the shotgun. Sully danced in a circle and whined. The dog seemed to know something was up. "Stay, Sully."

Hannah returned to the steps. She couldn't call the damned cops. She paused for a moment, eyeing their vehicles parked in the driveway. She could just find the keys and take off. Keep running.

No, she had to go in there. These people had been kind enough to offer her lodging. If only they knew what she was really like. A murderer.

Hannah approached the front door. She flipped on the lights. To her surprise, they came on. Maybe she'd seen too many horror movies where a psycho killer had cut the power.

"Jeremy? Kelly?"

No response came.

Hannah swept the downstairs, starting in the kitchen. Everything looked in place. The clean dinner dishes sat in the drainer. A dishtowel had been folded neatly and draped over the oven handle. Nothing amiss here.

She left the kitchen and checked out an office room with built-in shelves. A laptop rested on the desk. Some of Jeremy's books were stacked on the shelves. The room was mostly filled with cardboard boxes.

As she moved to a second downstairs room, she found a desk with another laptop. A notepad lay on the desk with some doodles on it. Nothing odd in this room.

No windows had been broken. After checking out the offices, she went to the back door and found it locked.

That left the upstairs.

Upstairs, she checked the first bedroom. The sheets were rumpled. The muddy prints continued on the carpet. "Hello?"

No answer came. She checked the other rooms upstairs, which were full of boxes. No sign of Jeremy or Kelly. She surmised they'd been forced from their house in a hurry. Their vehicles were still parked outside.

Was creepy Keppler involved? She would find out if he was home. Go over there with the shotgun. What did she have to lose? He wasn't about to call the cops on her.

Hannah returned to the garage apartment, where Sully greeted her by licking her hand. She sat on the bed and set the shotgun down. Sully nudged her leg, and she scratched behind his ears. The dog seemed to know something was amiss with his owners.

She felt mentally sharper, the pain pill having worn off. She gathered up her bag and the shotgun, then went back to the house with Sully in tow. Hannah searched the kitchen and found a bag of Purina dog food. She grabbed that and Sully's food and water dishes. No telling if she'd be back here, and she wasn't about to leave the dog.

Hannah threw some random snacks in her bag and found a set of car keys on the counter.

"C'mon Sully. Let's go find your mom and dad."

She drove down the road to Keppler's place. She parked at the end of the driveway and observed the house. It was dark and silent as a church in the evening. Keppler's pickup truck was parked near the house.

She waited a few moments, and when she saw no activity, Hannah pulled up near the house.

"Stay here, boy. Be right back," she said.

After grabbing the shotgun, she got out of the vehicle and climbed the steps. She peered in a window, checking out the living room. It appeared neat, if old fashioned. The couch was a flowered abomination from the eighties and Keppler had an oak entertainment center against one wall. No TV in it, but then she spotted a modern flat screen mounted on the wall.

She walked the wraparound porch, peering in windows. When she got to the side door, she tried it. Locked. Keppler appeared to have blown this particular pop stand.

For good measure, she checked the back door. If he happened to come out, he'd get the shotgun pointed in his face.

It occurred to her they might be inside. Going in the house

would be a huge risk, but she had to check. She managed to find an unlocked window off the porch. After looking around, she opened the window and wiggled inside, the shotgun tucked under her arm.

The place smelled like lemon furniture polish. The end tables and coffee table gleamed. The rug looked freshly vacuumed. She wouldn't have taken Keppler for neat and clean.

She explored the downstairs, moving through the kitchen, dining room, and an empty room with built-in bookshelves. No books on the shelves. Keppler wasn't a reader. She spotted a photo scrapbook tucked on the bottom shelf.

Hannah knelt and grabbed the scrapbook. Papers overflowed at its edges. She opened it up. There were newspaper clippings and printouts stuffed inside. The first yellowed news clipping detailed the murder of a prison inmate. Melvin Keppler was killed in Wende Correctional Facility. Beaten to death with a broken table leg. There was a picture of Melvin Keppler, and the resemblance to Richard Keppler was unmistakable. She found a second clipping. *Murdered Inmate's Wife Found Dead.*

Maryanne Keppler, wife of recently murdered inmate Henry Keppler, was found dead of an apparent overdose. Keppler had been the one to find her. It probably wouldn't have warranted a news story if she hadn't been married to the recently murdered Melvin.

There were other, equally disturbing clips. Mostly about missing women. They had all been abducted in New York, Pennsylvania, and Ohio. Some had been taken from rest stops. Two were taken in parking ramps. A few more had been on bike trails when they'd been snatched.

Keppler was even worse than she'd thought. A bona fide serial killer. Why else would he keep all these clippings? She put the book back on the shelf. She wanted to wash her hands.

Upstairs, she found one bedroom furnished. One thing she found odd was the lack of any pictures or artwork hung on the walls. The remaining upstairs rooms were wallpapered and blank. She decided to circle back to the kitchen, where she'd seen a cellar door.

Hannah opened the door and stared into the darkness. A set of wooden steps led into the basement. She found the light switch and flipped it. A series of fluorescents popped on. Hannah paused to listen. A furnace whooshed to life.

She descended and ended up in a narrow hallway. The walls were unfinished drywall, dotted with joint compound. Hannah proceeded and turned left. There were doors along the hallway.

Down on the right, she spotted a piece of plywood leaning against the wall. A few five-gallon buckets had been shoved against the plywood. Why stand a piece of plywood up like that? She pulled the plywood back and saw a heavy steel door behind it.

Keppler had padlocked the door. Something was in there. Maybe something she didn't want to see. She took a few moments to slide the buckets out of the way. Then she set the plywood aside.

The door had a basic padlock you could get at any hardware store. Using the shotgun's stock, she hammered the lock off with three solid blows. The lock clattered on the floor. She unlatched the door and paused for a moment.

Did she want to see what was behind the door? What if Jeremy and Kelly were in there?

Hannah pulled the door open. Stale air blew in her face. Under that was the smell of something rotten. Corrupt. She reached inside and found the light switch.

The light revealed a bloodstained table fitted with restraints. More brownish stains covered the floor. This is where he took his victims. Hannah fought back a gag. How many women had died terrified and hopeless in this room?

She turned off the light and backed out of the room. Then she spent a few minutes putting the plywood and buckets in place.

The lock was a loss. She shoved it behind the buckets.

Hannah wormed her way through the rest of the basement,

eventually ending up in a storm cellar. She pushed on the double storm doors. They were locked from the outside.

Keppler was gone.

He took them to the cabin. You know what you need to do.

Hannah returned to the SUV. As she opened the door, Sully greeted her with a WOOF! She set the shotgun on the floor in back, then rummaged through her bag for the dagger. Once it was in hand, she slashed the tires on Keppler's truck.

Should he return home, he wouldn't be going anywhere in the truck.

She hoped there was time. If Keppler had taken Jeremy and Kelly, he intended to keep them alive for a bit. She would've found bodies in their house if he'd intended to kill them quickly. Why them though? Abducting neighbors was a huge risk.

Hannah hurried to the borrowed vehicle and pulled out of Keppler's driveway.

The muscles in Jeremy's wrists and shoulders were a five alarm fire. His fingers tingled, and the glue from the duct tape tasted awful in his mouth. Those were the least of his worries. Keppler turned out to be more than just annoying and creepy. He was downright dangerous.

There'd been no warning. One moment he'd been asleep, and the next, the cold steel of the revolver had been pressed against his skull. He didn't own a firearm. Wasn't one to be paranoid and keep weapons stashed in the bedroom.

Even if he'd had a gun, Keppler was so physically imposing Jeremy doubted he'd have a chance.

He looked into Kelly's eyes and saw panic. He felt the same as his heart felt like it was trying to punch its way through his chest. He took some deep breaths through his nose.

Try and find a chance to escape. Maybe when he gets us out of this stinking RV. If nothing else, we might be able to outrun him if he cuts the tape.

Jeremy felt the RV slow, then turn. The engine groaned and the vehicle bumped over rough ground. Eventually, the RV came to a halt. He heard the seat groan as Keppler stood up. He craned his neck and looked up at Keppler. The giant seemed even bigger from down here.

"Wait here," Keppler said. "If you're in any different spot when I get back, I'll shoot your wife."

Keppler exited the RV's side door. Jeremy heard his footsteps crunch outside. He felt helpless.

They were completely fucked.

CHAPTER
THIRTEEN

KEPPLER WENT INSIDE THE CABIN. It stank of blood and death. He'd have to figure out how to keep the writer in one place. At some point, he'd have to leave the cabin for supplies. He'd figure that out.

Keppler returned to the RV. They'd behaved and hadn't moved. He knelt near the writer. "I'm going to cut your feet loose. We're going to take a walk. Understand?"

Jeremy nodded.

Keppler sawed through the duct tape around the writer's ankles. He grabbed the back of the writer's shirt and helped him up. He forced Jeremy inside the cabin and sat him in a kitchen chair. Then he ripped the tape from the writer's mouth.

"Let us go."

"Don't make me laugh."

"What do you want?"

"You're going to perform a task for me."

"What could I possibly do for you?"

"Write my story."

"What the hell story is that?"

"I want to be a legend."

He saw the bewildered look on Jeremy's face.

"Gacy. Bundy. Dahmer."

"You're a serial killer?"

"The FBI and the police would classify me that way."

"How many people have you killed?" Jeremy asked.

"North of twenty."

"And you're going to kill me?"

"Not if you do what I want."

"You just confessed to me though."

"You'll have to trust me."

"Where am I writing this book?"

"Here. I brought a typewriter and paper."

"I've never used a typewriter."

"You need to learn. A lot depends on it. Wait here. I'm going to get some stuff out of the RV."

Jeremy watched Keppler leave the cabin. He looked around. The place stank. Something he couldn't quite place. Like a butcher shop where meat went rancid. He spotted stains on the linoleum in the kitchen. They looked like blood. Was this Keppler's killing ground?

He had to figure a way to escape. Keppler had confessed to him, and it wasn't likely he'd leave here alive. There was one other room. A bathroom, he guessed. There probably wasn't a back door.

He sat there feeling weak and stupid. It had happened so fast. One moment he was sleeping and the next he'd had a gun to his head. You never think something like that will happen. And if it does, you imagine taking care of business, smashing the intruder with a bat or a golf club. Fending them off until the police arrive and you're a heroic homeowner.

Reality could be a pisser.

Kelly was out there with Keppler. He had to try and stop Keppler. God knew what he was doing out there.

As Jeremy stood up, Keppler trudged back inside. He carried

a plastic case with a handle and a ream of paper under his arm. Jeremy sat down. Keppler hadn't seemed to notice that Jeremy had stood up.

"What's that?"

"Your writing tool. The typewriter."

He'd been raised on laptops and smartphones. Jeremy didn't even know you could still buy a typewriter anymore.

Keppler set it on the kitchen table. He thumped the ream of paper down next to the typewriter.

"What am I supposed to write?"

"I'll dictate. You type."

"Why do you want me to write this down?"

"I want my story told. Someday, I'll send it to the media, or maybe a publisher. Guys like Gacy and Bundy are famous. Maybe they'll make a movie about me."

"Those guys were sick fucks."

"You saying I'm sick?"

"You did tell me you've killed people."

"Society is sick. My parents were sick. I'm just a product of that. A symptom of a disease."

"And if I do this, you'll let us go?"

"You have my word."

"Did you hurt Kelly?"

"She's right as rain."

"Why isn't she in here?" Jeremy said.

Keppler sat down across from him. The chair looked like the tiny seats you see in elementary school classrooms in comparison to Keppler's size. "She'll stay out there. You do what I want, she'll be fine. You don't, I'll have to take it out on your wife."

Jeremy closed his eyes, exhaled. "I don't have a choice. I'll do it."

"Good. We'll get started shortly."

KEPPLER'S STORY

Legends

The Story of Richard Keppler

I'm going to pass into legend. Become one of the legends that haunts people. The subject of articles and podcasts. Mentioned in the same breath as guys like Ed Gein. I guess I've always had the urge. Most of my fantasies revolved around killing my parents. That started around seven years old.

My father caught me with a comic book. He thought they were trash. The X-Men. He'd told me to throw it out, but I didn't. I got the belt across the back for that. After he whipped me, I laid on my bed and cried. It left welts. The welts turned to bruises. I imagined tying him up, then getting some gasoline from the garage. Pouring it on him and lighting it up. He would've screamed really loud.

I wouldn't have cared if the whole house had burned down. I hated the place.

When I was ten, my father decided to build a bunch of rooms and hallways in our basement. I helped him, soaking in his whiskey stink as he muttered and swore while sawing lumber or hammering nails. He punched me in the arm if I was too slow to bring him a tool. Or slapped the back of my head. That was one of his favorites.

He had no reason to build rooms in the basement. Those rooms served me well later in life. Like everything my father did, there was no rhyme or reason. He never spent time in the basement. Mostly he sat at the kitchen table and sipped whiskey after work. Or watched television alone and drank beer. That's when the whiskey was gone.

Once those rooms were built, my mother was the only person who went down there. And that was to do laundry.

He beat the shit out of my mother really bad. The beatings were normal, but one time he went too far. The cops took him away and he got sent to Wende. Another inmate beat him to death with a table leg. The other inmate didn't like my father's charges. The fact that he'd put his hands on a woman.

I found my mother dead not too long after my father got killed. She drank herself into a stupor, puked, and choked on it. She was in the bathroom, yellow-green vomit crusted on her mouth. Her skin was blue. The coroner ruled it death by misadventure and I got the house.

Six months later, I killed someone.

After listening to Keppler's story, Jeremy wanted to bleach his brain, get the filth out. Keppler had sat across from him, spewing out his story. Now, Keppler was pacing in the kitchen.

"That's enough for a chapter?"

"A chapter can really be any length, but yeah."

"That's a good start."

"Is Kelly comfortable in the RV?"

"She's fine."

"Did you untie her?"

"Do I look stupid?"

Keppler continued pacing. The floor squeaked under his weight.

"We were tied up in an awkward position."

"I'm not concerned about that. I have to go somewhere. Get on the ground."

He dreaded being bound with the tape again. Didn't have much choice, though.

"On your belly."

He got on his stomach and Keppler bound his wrists and ankles, the same way he'd done in the RV.

"You've cooperated, so I won't put tape over your mouth."

Keppler left the cabin. Jeremy heard the lock click. He rocked back and forth, which did no good. He strained his wrists against the tape, but he'd been tied tight. Same with his ankles.

All he could do was wait.

CHAPTER
FOURTEEN

KEPPLER RETURNED TO THE RV. Kelly lay on her stomach, right where he'd left her. He stood over her. She looked up at him, eyes pleading. He'd seen that look dozens of times from his victims. That look when they knew nothing was going to save them.

He rolled her over and scooped her up. She struggled against him. "Stop moving or I'll drop you."

Keppler carried her to the rear bedroom. He set her on the bed and shut the bifold door. No one would see her back there. Perfect while he ran his errand.

Back in the driver's seat, he started it up and hit the road. He was headed back to Home Depot. He initially hadn't thought of something. The writer would need to be restrained while Keppler was running errands, and duct tape wouldn't always be convenient.

He reached the home improvement store and parked away from the other cars. Then he checked on Kelly, who lay on the bed.

"Don't make any noise. I'll be right back."

She muttered something under the tape, but he couldn't tell what she'd said.

Keppler went inside and purchased a heavy chain and a large eye hook. One he could screw into a stud. He also bought a heavy carabiner clip, and a sturdy padlock. Keppler took his purchases to the register and paid for them.

One more stop. There was a sex shop down the road in one of the strip plazas called *Enchanted Delights*. They sold all sorts of kinky BDSM shit in there. It would be perfect.

He parked outside the shop and went inside. The walls were lined with packaged dildoes, butt plugs, and vibrators. The rear of the store housed DVDs with categories ranging from Lesbian to Asian. He found the BDSM stuff and purchased some cuffs and a dog collar with a sturdy clasp.

He paid for the items and left the store.

Once he was back in the cabin, he left Jeremy bound on the floor and went to work. After about ten minutes, he'd screwed the eye hook into a stud and attached the chain to it with the carabiner clip. He fastened the collar around Jeremy's neck. The cuffs would keep his arms restrained.

This setup was better than constantly duct taping Jeremy.

"What am I, a dog?"

"Ensures you won't try and escape."

"Where's Kelly?"

"She's in the RV. Don't worry, she's fine."

"I want to see her."

"Not possible."

"Is she alive?"

"She is."

"When do you want me to start the next chapter?"

"After I get some groceries. Have to keep you fed if I want you to tell my story. First, let's keep you secure."

• • •

The collar chafed his neck. Jeremy could never stand anything around his throat. He even hated having a turtleneck on. Not that he'd worn one since he was a kid. Swallowing seemed tougher. He sat on the floor near the wall, hands cuffed behind his back. He decided to stand up.

Keppler had secured the chain to the collar with a padlock. Jeremy tugged at it, but it wouldn't give.

He'd given some thought to trying to yank the eye bolt and chain from the wall. That might cause him to bust his windpipe and die suffocating on a stinking cabin floor. He settled for sitting on the floor near the kitchen table.

Maybe Hannah had seen something and called the cops. He was thankful Sully had been with her during the abduction. Something told him Keppler wouldn't have been kind to their pet. Hopefully Hannah was caring for the dog.

He could refuse to write any more until Keppler let him see Kelly. She could already be dead, a possibility he didn't want to fathom. If she was gone, he'd want to be dead, as well.

He heard the RV engine. His host had returned.

Hannah found a dirt path down the road from Keppler's cabin and parked about halfway down. She was sure no one could see the vehicle from the road. She leashed Sully and let him out to take care of business. He lifted his leg and marked a nearby tree.

She poured some bottled water in his dish and Sully lapped it up. Hannah was glad to have the dog for company, but she felt a huge weight. She had to care for the dog. For something else other than herself. For years, she'd been on her own. After Derek, she'd given up on relationships and resigned to living solo.

Being called a silly bitch and having a rib cracked after one of his rages tended to do that. She liked the dog. Dogs in general. They were loyal. They loved you unconditionally. And a good dog wouldn't fuck you over or hurt you. Unlike Derek or her sainted father.

Sully woofed. He'd drained the water from the bowl. She put it back in the car, then urged Sully into the back seat. "Stay here bud."

The cabin was off to her right. The thick trees provided a buffer between her and the structure. She should be able to have a look and remain concealed. Once Sully was in the car, she grabbed the shotgun and crept through the woods.

She hunkered behind a thick tree trunk a hundred yards from the cabin. The RV was parked out front. He was here. No other vehicles around.

Hannah watched the cabin for a few minutes. Keppler stepped outside. He climbed in the RV. A moment later he emerged carrying two grocery bags. He planned on being here for a while. Were the groceries just for him? Or were Jeremy and Kelly inside?

Hannah watched the cabin for another twenty minutes, noticing no movement. She could come back tonight under cover of darkness and observe Keppler.

If Jeremy and Kelly were in there, she'd get them out.

CHAPTER
FIFTEEN

THE TYPEWRITER WAS a pain in the ass. Jeremy had figured it out, but he'd been spoiled by modern technology. Making corrections was a bitch. He forced himself to slow down. He could usually crank out a thousand words an hour on his laptop. Sometimes more if he was writing hot.

Keppler had brought food. He'd had some crackers with spray can cheese and a granola bar. Not exactly gourmet food. After eating, he'd typed another chapter. Keppler dictated. This chapter was about Keppler's high school fantasies. He'd dreamt of kidnapping his economics teacher and torturing her in the basement.

Keppler also had wild fantasies of killing classmates who picked on him for his weight and acne. Pushing kids downstairs. Smashing faces into lockers. Having access to a diseased mind made Jeremy's stomach feel greasy.

Keppler let him take a break after he wrote two more chapters.

"Did Kelly eat?" Jeremy asked.

"I gave her something."

"Are you going to read this chapter?"

"In a minute."

"Can I see Kelly? I've been cooperating with you."

"You want to know she's okay?"

"I'd be able to work faster knowing she's okay."

"Fair enough. Be right back."

Keppler headed outside. He heard the RV's door bang. A moment later, the screaming started.

It was Kelly. Jeremy wasn't restrained, and he ran out the door. Kelly's scream rose to a crescendo. From inside the RV, she begged Keppler to stop. He was going to kill that son of a bitch. Leaving him unchained would be Keppler's last mistake.

As Keppler stepped from the RV's door, Jeremy charged him. Head lowered, he slammed his shoulder into Keppler's gut. Keppler didn't budge. He picked Jeremy up and slammed him on the ground. The wind popped from his lungs.

Jesus, that was like slamming into a concrete pillar.

Jeremy rolled around, gasping, the wind knocked out of him.

After a few moments, air flooded into his lungs. What a relief. Keppler pointed the revolver at him.

"Stand up."

Jeremy's back ached from being slammed. That was going to hurt even worse in the morning. He got to his feet.

"I was doing you a favor," Keppler said.

Jeremy pictured himself launching a brick at Keppler's face. "What did you do to her?"

"Gave you proof she's alive. You heard her, right?"

"Fuck you, you freak."

"Hold out your hand. Palm up."

"Why should I do that?"

"If you don't, I'll go back in there and make her scream more."

Jeremy complied and held out his hand.

Keppler reached into his pocket and plucked something out. He dropped it in Jeremy's palm. Jeremy regarded it for a moment. It took a second before he realized it was one of Kelly's fingernails.

His stomach went sour. A surge of adrenaline shot through him, leaving him shaking. He was no match for Keppler. Not without a weapon. "Don't hurt her again."

"Are you satisfied she's alive?"

"You're a sick son of a bitch."

"Watch what you say. I can bring you other proof she's still alive. Back inside."

Inside the cabin, Keppler chained Jeremy up. He glanced out the window. Darkness settled outside. It was a deep, solid blackness, unlit by streetlights. He thought of Kelly, scared and alone in the RV. There was nothing he could've done to prevent this. Keppler was like a freak storm that pummeled a city with multiple feet of snow. He just happened.

He still had to figure a way out of here.

Keppler sat at the kitchen table. He shoveled Ritz crackers into his face. Crumbs fell onto his shirt, but he didn't seem to care. He stared at the sleeve of crackers, as if in deep thought.

"I'm hungry," Jeremy said. "Can I get something to eat."

Keppler kept munching crackers.

"I said I'm hungry."

"I heard you."

"Well?"

"No dinner for you. Not after you attacked me."

"You want me to be able to concentrate on writing. Food helps."

"I should cut something off and make you eat it."

"That might affect my ability to write."

"Do you think I could do it?" Keppler said, looking at Jeremy. Cracker crumbs dotted his chin.

"I think you're capable of a lot of things."

Keppler regarded him with a flat gaze. "I'm glad you understand that. You still get no food until morning."

"Do you want me to write another chapter?"

"Not tonight."

Jeremy tugged at the collar. "Can you take this chain off so I can sleep tonight?"

"No," Keppler said. "Part of the punishment. No more talking."

He turned back to his crackers. He ate another, crunching away as the crumbs cascaded down his shirt.

Sleep would be impossible with the collar around his neck. He sat against the wall near the table, drew his knees up.

He'd watch Keppler, wait for his chance. There had to be a way out of this.

Hannah had waited in the car most of the day, letting Sully out when he needed to handle business. Now that night had fallen, she was going to take another look at the cabin. She cracked the windows in the car for Sully, who had curled up on the back seat.

After grabbing the shotgun, she snuck up on the property. She hunkered among the trees. Keppler had no spotlights on the cabin's exterior. That worked in her favor. The RV stood there, no light coming from its exterior.

She slipped out of the woods and scurried to the RV. Rounded it and eased the door open. Hannah slinked inside. It smelled like a dirty sock. Brown stains dotted the orange carpet.

Hannah spotted a bifold door at the rear of the vehicle. She slipped past the kitchenette and paused at the door. Hannah whipped the door open, stepped back, and raised the shotgun.

Kelly lay on the bed. Her hands and feet were bound. Tape had been slapped over her mouth. Blood coated one of her hands. She was on her side. Kelly's eyes grew wide at seeing Hannah.

Hannah knelt on the bed. She removed the tape from Kelly's mouth.

"Where's Keppler?"

"In the cabin," Kelly said. "How'd you know it was him."

Hannah tossed the wad of tape aside. "Did some detective work. Where's your husband?"

"I think Keppler's got him in there."

"Your hand's bleeding."

"That son of a bitch ripped out my fingernail."

Hannah took her knife and sliced through Kelly's bonds. Hannah balled up the tape and threw it on the floor. Kelly sat up and shook her hands, trying to improve the circulation.

"Pins and needles," Kelly said.

Her finger was an ugly purple-red where the nail had been removed.

"Why'd he rip out your nail?"

"Didn't say. Just came in and did it."

As Hannah shifted off the bed, Pain lit through her side. She doubled over and let out a groan.

"You okay?"

"Cancer's acting up."

"You serious?"

"Unfortunately. Had breast cancer. It's come roaring back and metastasized."

"I'm so sorry. That's awful," Kelly said, putting a hand on her arm.

"Got a shitty break. Not the first person it's ever happened to," Hannah said. "We need to find Jeremy and get you out of here."

"Where'd the gun come from?"

"Long story. C'mon," Hannah said.

Hannah headed to the RV's front and regarded the cabin out the windshield. No lights on. She didn't see any movement in the windows. Maybe busting inside with the gun and shocking Keppler would be the best plan. Especially if he was sleeping.

"I'm going in," Hannah said.

"I can't let you do that."

"Do you have a better idea?"

"Call the cops."

That wasn't gonna happen. "Might be too late for that."

"You going to shoot him?"

"I'll see what happens," Hannah said.

"Do you have another gun?"

"Just this one. And my knife."

"Give me the knife," Kelly said.

"You sure?"

"It's *my* husband in there."

Hannah handed her the knife.

"Looks damned sharp."

"It is."

Hannah didn't want to tell her what it had been used for.

"Off we go then."

Outside the cabin, they ducked below the window. She assumed the front door would be locked. Hannah listened outside the front door. No footsteps or creaking boards sounded within.

She considered blasting the door. That might put Jeremy at risk, as she didn't know his location. Might not take care of the lock, either.

As she was pondering how to enter, the door flew open. Keppler stood in the doorway. His eyes grew wide. As he reached in his pocket, Hannah raised the shotgun. Keppler ducked out of the doorway. She fired, blasting a chunk out of the door frame.

Gunshots popped from inside the cabin. Hannah and Kelly scrambled. She hadn't counted on Keppler having a gun.

They retreated to the RV. Hannah slammed the door. She heard Keppler coming, his footfalls thumping. They'd pissed off an angry giant, just like Jack of beanstalk fame.

"If you come out now, I won't kill him."

It sounded like he was right outside the door.

Hannah racked the shotgun. The spent shell tumbled onto the rug.

"Are you coming out?" Keppler said.

Hannah fired through the door. She heard Keppler howl in pain. She racked the gun again, then kicked the door open. Stood there for a moment. Keppler lay on the ground. He'd been gut shot. The blood spread on his shirt like a gruesome ink blot.

He moaned and held his belly, which only served to stain his hands with blood. Keppler's chrome revolver lay on the ground next to him.

Hannah stepped down, keeping the shotgun on Keppler.

Kelly slipped past her and scooped up the revolver.

Keppler looked at his wound. "You shot me."

"I'm going to check on Jeremy," Kelly said, and hurried into the cabin.

"It hurts," Keppler said. "Call an ambulance."

"How many?"

"What?"

"How many did you kill? I saw the room in your basement."

"You were in my house?"

"I was. How many women? I'm assuming it's women. It always is with you assholes."

"Twenty plus," Keppler said with a grin. Blood bubbled from his mouth.

"You don't deserve an ambulance."

Jeremy had watched Keppler rise from the couch and go to the door. Then the shooting had started. From his position in the cabin, he couldn't see who was out there. Thought maybe it was the cops.

He was stunned a few minutes later when Kelly charged inside.

She knelt near him, the two of them holding an embrace. Her tears dampened his face. Jeremy's throat tightened. After she broke off the hug, he took her injured hand in his. "How bad is it?"

"Hurts, but I'll live."

"Did he do anything else besides the fingernail?"

"No. That was more than enough."

"What happened out there?"

"Hannah came back for us. She shot him. He's lying in the grass."

"Good. I'll be needing the key for this padlock."

"I'll see if he has it.."

Outside, a gunshot boomed, causing Jeremy and Kelly to flinch. They exchanged a meaningful look. "I hope that was Hannah doing the shooting."

"I'll have a look."

Keppler had one last gasp in him. As he'd tried to sit up, Hannah pulled the trigger. He flopped back in the grass, the left half of his jaw now missing. But he was dead. No doubt there. A miserable dog put down. He wouldn't be hurting any more women.

She spotted Kelly standing in the cabin's doorway.

"Is he?"

"He's gone," Hannah said.

"I need a padlock key to free Jeremy."

Hannah resigned herself to digging through Keppler's pockets. After rifling through the left pocket, she switched to the right and breathed a sigh of relief when she touched metal. She pulled the padlock key out.

Kelly stepped off the cabin's porch and Hannah tossed her the key.

She looked down at Keppler. His tongue lolled on his ruined jaw like a slimy, pink slug. It was too much for Hannah. The back of her throat felt sour. Her stomach kicked, and she vomited in the grass. To top it off, the pain corkscrewed into her side again. When she was done puking, she wiped her mouth with the back of her hand.

What a crazy couple of days this had been. She'd left a body count in her wake. The sour taste of vomit lingered in her mouth. She spat on the grass. Keppler didn't seem the type to have an after dinner mint handy. She'd have to rinse the taste out of her mouth with some bottled water.

She headed to the cabin to check on Kelly and Jeremy.

Kelly popped the lock open and Jeremy removed the chain from the collar. Then he unfastened the collar. His neck felt chafed and raw. That was enough of being chained like a dog.

Kelly helped him up.

"What did he want from you?"

Jeremy pointed to the typewriter. "Wanted me to write his biography. Got a few chapters done."

"A real bestseller, huh?"

"Someone who likes all that serial killer crap would probably like it. True crime and all that."

"A typewriter. Old school."

"Guessing he didn't want any record of it on a computer or in the cloud."

"What kind of stuff?"

"Sick shit. Glad I didn't have to finish it."

Jeremy noticed Hannah standing in the doorway. "What now?"

"We should call the cops."

"Looks like he has other stuff in his pockets. Did he take your phones?"

"He did," Kelly said.

They went out and rummaged through Keppler's pockets.

Jeremy found their cell phones. His had around ten percent battery left.

"I need a head start," Hannah said.

"Head start where?" Kelly said.

"The police will want to talk to me."

Kelly said, "This was self defense. No way they'll charge you."

"Not him," Hannah said. "I'm in some other trouble."

"I'm sure they'll understand," Kelly said.

"Not so sure. Look, Sully's in your truck. He's doing good. Brought his food and water."

"Thank Christ. That was my next question," Kelly said.

"So can you wait a bit to call the cops?"

Kelly said, "What did you do?"

"Best if I don't get into it."

"Least we can do," Jeremy said. "You saved our ass."

"Sully's waiting. I'll take you there."

At the SUV, Hannah opened the door and Sully bounded out, running to Jeremy and Kelly, tail swishing. *Oh to feel that much joy.* Kelly knelt and hugged Sully, who licked her face as if she wore bacon-scented perfume. Jeremy joined in, scratching behind Sully's ears.

"Thanks for taking care of him," Jeremy said.

"He's a good dog."

Jeremy said, "Your car. You going to walk to town?"

Kelly stood up. "We can drive you to town."

Hannah shook her head. "You need to wait here for the cops."

"The RV runs," Jeremy said. "Just a thought."

Why not add grand theft auto to her rap sheet? "I suppose Keppler won't miss it."

"You'd best get that head start. We should call the police soon," Jeremy said. "We'll cover your tracks the best we can."

"I appreciate that. I'd better get moving," Hannah said.

Hannah returned to the cabin and found the RV keys on the counter. She snatched the bags of groceries Keppler had bought, as well. She hopped in the vehicle and started it up. She turned it around and headed down the road.

She had to find another place to stay. Another motel far from here. She'd put some distance between herself and the cabin, find a cheap motel somewhere. There'd be no more hunting down men. Hannah felt she'd done the ultimate good deed by saving Jeremy and Kelly. Maybe that'd be worth something at the end of her life.

On second thought, fuck motels. Maybe she'd just leave the car behind and take the RV on the road. Live out her days a nomad. What did she have to lose?

There was one less creep in the world with Keppler gone. As she drove, the pain in her side flared, the cancer making its presence known. She steadied the RV with one hand on the wheel until the pain passed.

She'd take it one day at a time. Try and spend her remaining days at peace. Maybe find a nice spot somewhere out in the woods where no one would bother her. Park the RV and remain a hermit with the time she had left.

She wasn't going to prison. If it came down to it, she had the pills and the shotgun.

There you go being morbid again.

Right now, all she wanted to do was rest her head. First, there were miles to go and plenty of distance to put between her and her crimes.

She looked forward to having some semblance of peace.

ABOUT THE AUTHOR

Anthony Izzo is the author of 40 horror and dark fiction titles. He enjoys writing tales of mayhem involving anything from zombies to psycho killers to murderous shapeshifters. Anthony has also served as a judge for the Buffalo Dreams Film Festival screenplay competition. Anthony holds a B.A. in English from D'Youville College in Buffalo, NY. When not writing, he likes playing loud guitar, reading, drawing, and spending time with family. He makes his home in the Western New York Area.

Check out Anthony's website at www.anthonyizzo.com

www.ingramcontent.com/pod-product-compliance
Lightning Source LLC
Chambersburg PA
CBHW052115150726
48002CB00006B/2358